*Also by* Kazumi Yumoto

THE FRIENDS

THE SPRING TONE

The
Letters

# The Letters

KAZUMI YUMOTO

TRANSLATED BY CATHY HIRANO

Farrar Straus Giroux * New York

Copyright © 1997 by Kazumi Yumoto
Translation copyright © 2002 by Farrar, Straus and Giroux
All rights reserved
Originally published in Japan under the title *Popura no aki* by Shinchosha
English translation rights arranged with Kazumi Yumoto
through Japan Foreign-Rights Centre
Distributed in Canada by Douglas & McIntyre Ltd.
Printed in the United States of America
Designed by Robbin Gourley
First American edition, 2002
10  9  8  7  6  5  4  3  2  1

Library of Congress Cataloging-in-Publication Data
Yumoto, Kazumi.
     [Popura no aki. English]
     The letters / Kazumi Yumoto ; translated by Cathy Hirano.—
1st American ed.
        p. cm.
     Summary: In Japan, the death of her former landlady triggers a young
woman's memories about her father's death when she was six years old,
and the special way the old lady helped her to cope with the loss.
     ISBN 0-374-34383-7
     [1. Death—Fiction.   2. Grief—Fiction.   3. Old-age—Fiction.
4. Letters—Fiction.   5. Landlord and tenant—Fiction.]   I. Hirano,
Cathy.   II. Title.

PZ7.K216 Le 2002
[Fic]—dc21

                                                              2001059768

# The Letters

## Chapter 1

WHAT'S WRONG? . . . You don't sound very cheerful. Have you eaten supper yet? . . . No, wait. I'm calling for a reason. I just got a call from Miss Sasaki . . . Yes, that's right. The woman from Poplar House."

As I listen to my mother speaking on the other end of the line, the years we spent in Poplar House come flooding back, and suddenly, I know. The old lady is dead.

By "the old lady," I mean Mrs. Yanagi, the landlady of the apartment where my mother and I lived for three years. My father died when I was six, and a short while later we were forced to leave our house. We moved to Poplar House, into one of three small apartments the old lady rented out. Miss Sasaki, the woman who had contacted my mother, also lived there.

"When Miss Sasaki dropped by to see her in the morning, there was no response. She seems to have died in her sleep."

"In the morning?"

"*This* morning."

I inhale slowly. If it was this morning, then even if she had come to my bedside to bid me farewell, I would have slept right through it. For some reason, when I knock myself out with pills at night, I am occasionally afflicted with powerful nightmares. Last night I dreamed that I was the corpse of an enormous fish being beaten against a concrete wall. It is a recurring pattern in my dreams.

"How old was she?" I ask.

"Ninety-eight. A peaceful way to go, don't you think?"

Which means that she must have been eighty when we lived there. Yet she had promised me when I was seven that she would try to stay alive until I grew up, and she had kept her word, although it must have required quite a firm resolve from someone as old as eighty.

"She said she called because there are some letters."

"Some what?"

My mother lowers her voice slightly and repeats slowly and distinctly, "Let-ters."

"Did Miss Sasaki say that?"

"Yes," my mother replies, but then changes the subject. "I wonder if I should send flowers . . ."

I was ten years old when we left Poplar House after my mother decided to remarry. Neither she nor I had seen our former landlady since, although of course we wrote letters and even sent the occasional photograph. But I know with absolute certainty that those are not the kind of letters Miss Sasaki was talking about. They are the letters I entrusted to the landlady when I was seven, the ones she had placed in a certain drawer of her black dresser. So she had kept them for me all this time.

"You send the flowers, Mom."

"Huh?"

"I'm going to the funeral. It won't take long by plane."

"Won't the hospital mind?"

It has been a month since I quit working as a nurse at the hospital, but I still haven't told my mother. "Don't worry about that."

"Who said I was worrying?" Then, after a short silence, she adds, "You always make your own decisions anyway."

"That's right."

"Say hello to Miss Sasaki for me."

"Sure."

After hanging up the phone, I sit staring vacantly for a while. What a long distance now separates me from our old landlady and Poplar House and the poplar tree in the yard, from everything that I had once thought "good," although I am not sure what that meant. It is as if the three years plus that I spent in Poplar House have become no more than a dream to the person I am now.

I throw a change of underwear and some toiletries and a paper bag full of medicine into an overnight bag and firmly zip it shut. I mutter to myself that it is ridiculous to take all my sleeping pills with me when I'll only be gone for one or two days, but another part of my brain retorts, "You don't think it's ridiculous at all. You know you can't get it off your mind." I shake my head. I don't know what will happen after this, but I do know that tonight at least I am not going to let myself be a dead fish. And tomorrow I will get on the plane and pay my respects to the old lady. That much I have to do.

I crawl under the covers and close my eyes. I hear rustling poplar leaves whisper in my ear. "Let's talk. Let's talk," they say. It is a pleasant, dry autumn sound, and I know immediately that it does not come from outside.

*Chapter 2*

WHEN THE FIRST RUSH of activity had passed following my father's death in a car accident, my mother seemed to carry on with the housework as usual. Then suddenly she stopped and went to sleep. She slept and slept. How long did it last, I wonder? A week? It seems much longer, but perhaps it was only three or four days. I was still in first grade. All I remember is that before I knew it, the summer vacation had already started, and I was eating canned salmon whenever I felt hungry while my mother slept. It seems odd that there was nothing in the cupboard but cans of fish. The salmon on the label had a cold glassy stare, and it certainly was not someone I could talk to. I haven't been able to stomach canned salmon since, and even now, when I see stacks of it displayed in the grocery store, the soles of my feet turn clammy.

By the time I had consumed a lifetime's worth of salmon in a matter of days, my mother got up with the same abruptness with which she had taken to her bed. Now she began riding the commuter trains, taking me with her. It was not as if she was going anywhere. She just boarded whatever train happened to come along, then rode and rode until she decided to get off. Under the scorching summer sun, we would traipse about some town that we had never seen before, stop somewhere to eat cold noodles or crushed ice with syrup, and then board a train once again.

I don't think we talked much during that time. I was well aware that my mother had no desire to speak about my father. As for myself, although the news that he was dead had at first filled me with grief—and I had wept aloud when I saw him lying in the coffin, his head bandaged in white gauze—now I felt as though a membrane had stretched itself around my heart, and I could no longer recall what my father was like when he was alive. The tremendous grief that my mother nursed as anger and rejection of the world around her had communicated itself to me as well.

We returned home exhausted every evening and collapsed onto our futons, which we didn't bother to fold up and put away, and fell into a deep sleep. I have no happy memories of that time. I merely hoped that if we maintained this daily routine, my mother would somehow survive. At six years of age, that was my only thought; that and the fact that this was a one-hundred-percent improvement over eating canned salmon every day.

Whatever the case, it was thanks to this train riding that we found Poplar House. One day we had been riding an empty train through the suburbs for some time when, just by chance, we got off at a particular station. The platform overlooked a river, and we walked to the end of it, squinting against the bright glare of the sun reflected off the concrete. The river, the grass, the bridge, and even the dusty earth seemed bleached by the merciless sun. A thin trickle of water flowed weakly in the riverbed, but the sky seemed enormous. It made me feel like saying, "Well, hey now, would you look at that!" I drew a deep breath.

"Shall we go through the ticket gate and take a look?" my mother asked. I was startled. Not once since our commuter train tour began had she consulted me about which train to get on or where to get off. "Don't you want to?"

I shook my head hurriedly. "No, I don't mind." And then, with a solemn feeling of responsibility, I began to walk beside her, staring straight ahead as she strode along briskly.

Passing through a shopping arcade, we came to a fire station. A creek ran alongside the road in front of it, and we followed this endlessly through a monotonous residential area. It must have been about two in the afternoon. There was no shade along the road by the creek, and the sun beat down so intensely it seemed to obliterate even sound. Not a cicada hummed, not a human stirred, not a bird flew, and I had finished the last drop of water in my thermos long ago. Falling behind my mother, I concentrated solely on placing one foot in front of the other, staring fixedly at her back. When she suddenly stopped and said, "Let's go over there," my brain was no longer functioning, and my feet just kept moving automatically so that my forehead with my sweat-soaked bangs plastered to it collided with her soft rump. I looked up to where she was pointing. "Over there. That tree. It's huge, isn't it?"

"It sure is," I agreed. A treetop higher than a telephone pole burst out between the roofs, towering above us. There was not a breath of wind, yet the leaves up there swayed gently, and I felt the perspiration on my brow recede just looking at it.

"Let's go to where that tree is."

I nodded. "Okay."

"Chiaki, you're drenched with sweat. Is there anything left in your thermos?"

"I drank it all already. But I'm okay." Once again I felt that I must show my mettle, and I started off ahead of my mother. After following the road by the creek a little farther, we turned our backs to it and went down a narrow lane barely wide enough for a single car to pass along, and immediately spotted the yard that belonged to the huge tree. It was certainly not a well-ordered, neatly weeded garden, nor was it pathetically overcrowded or ornately designed. And it definitely was not a wasteland. It was obvious that it had grown this way thanks only to the passage of time and a certain amount of faithful weeding, and that the gardener had no further ambitions whatsoever. There was a maple tree thick with green leaves, an oleander with red flowers stretching its arms toward the roof of the neighbor's shed, a Japanese laurel with glossy leaves, and a spirea that sprawled over the ground. Orange lilies poked their faces up here and there without logical connection. A blue porcelain brazier, looking most content, sat serenely upon the earth. And in the middle of the yard, its leaves ruffled occasionally by a gentle puff of air, stood the great tree. As I gazed up at it, I felt like sitting down on the spot and falling asleep.

"Chiaki. Chiaki." My mother beckoned to me. "I found out what kind of tree it is."

"What is it?"

"It's a poplar." She pointed. One of the gateposts, which were made of concrete blocks, bore a white porcelain nameplate. "Poplar Co-op," it said. The name sounded funny to me, and I rolled it over in my mouth. "Pop-lar Co-op. Pop-lar Co-op."

My mother began muttering to herself again. "It doesn't

look like an ordinary house. The upstairs rooms are apartments."

The building was a wooden structure with a rather unimposing set of apartments on the second floor. A flight of stairs ran up the outside of the building on the north side, facing the road along the creek. Three doors opened onto the balcony, and there were washing machines beside two of them.

"Chiaki, how would you like to live here?" This second question of the day was so unexpected that I was at a loss for words. Following my mother's gaze, I saw a cardboard sign hanging from the open iron gate. "Room for rent."

"Room for rent?"

"It means they want someone to move here." I thought this was not a bad idea at all. I had been vaguely aware that we would have to move out of the house we had been living in, and besides, I had fallen in love with the garden.

"If you want to, it's all right with me, Mom."

"What about *you*, Chiaki?"

"I think it's a good idea." My mother scrutinized my face closely and then walked briskly through the gate without any further hesitation.

The apartment layout was fairly typical. The kitchen area was situated on one side of the front door, which faced north, and the bath and toilet on the other side, followed by a small room with a wooden floor, and then a slightly larger room with sun-faded straw tatami mats on the south side of the building. Carrying only what would fit into this limited space, we moved in. Without the least sign of regret, my mother disposed of everything but the bare necessities. And she performed every action, from deciding on our new home to getting rid of our old house, with a swiftness that belied her normally sedate character.

There were only three apartments, all on the second floor. Miss Sasaki, a single woman who worked for a garment company, lived in the apartment closest to the west side where the gate was. Mr. Nishioka, a taxi driver, also single, lived in the middle. And my mother and I became the residents of the apartment at the back of the house, right at the top of the stairs.

The landlady lived alone on the first floor. She had rebuilt the house and added the apartments when her husband, a professor of Chinese literature, died. I learned later that the name "Poplar Co-op" was the invention of the real estate agent who found her first tenants. The landlady wanted to call it "Poplar House," but he advised her that "Poplar Co-op" sounded more sophisticated. By the time we moved there, however, the residents, neighbors, and even the mailman called it "Poplar House."

The landlady seemed like a rather unapproachable character to me. I admit that at the same time I felt some degree of fascination, something akin to the powerful urge to gaze upon the macabre, although I was almost too scared to look. She was absolutely terrifying.

Her round, deeply wrinkled forehead was broad and protruding. Her chin tilted upward, perhaps because she had no teeth except the three front ones on the bottom. It would be an understatement to say that her crumpled face merely resembled Popeye's, for she was in fact his spitting image. Except, that is, for the sharp, beady eyes that peered out from the depths of the crevice between her forehead and her cheeks. Those eyes were sufficient evidence for me that her true identity was Popeye transformed into a villain by some dubious potion.

The inside of her house, too, was spooky enough to scare any child. Perhaps she abhorred sunlight, for only one shutter had been opened. Peering into the gloomy darkness of her house from the entranceway on that first day when the poplar tree had beckoned us to it, we could see a wall covered with old books and a stone dragon glaring at us. A red talisman, inscribed with indecipherable Chinese characters for who knows what charm or incantation and stuck near the ceiling in the hallway, was the sort of vivid color that could appear only in a bad dream.

The root cause of my fear, however, was far more practical. She told us right from the beginning that she would not accept children. Although she relented and allowed us to move there, I was very anxious not to do anything to displease her in case she threw us out. Although it was just an apartment, to me it represented a sanctuary attained only after a seemingly endless stream of canned salmon and commuter trains.

My mother went out job-hunting daily. I spent the weeks at the end of that summer on my own, just gazing out the window at the poplar tree, completely absorbed in its swaying leaves, the birds that flocked to it, the shadows between its overlapping leaves, which changed with the angle of the sun. When I ate the two balls of rice my mother had made for my lunch, I ate them facing the tree. When the landlady, a hand towel tied like a scarf around her head, came out in the early evening, placed a mosquito coil at her feet, and began to weed, I still kept watching the poplar, although I retreated slightly from the window so that she would not see me. It was not as if I actually talked to the tree, but I don't remember ever feeling bored or lonely. When I look back on it, I have not had such a peaceful summer since. Even now, my image of summer consists of shadows darkening and deepening as the light intensifies, and the quietness those shadows envelop.

These quiet days came to an end in September when I went back to school. Not to the private girls' school that I had previously attended, but to the public elementary school near Poplar House. Of course, there was the problem of distance, but more practically, I think the monthly fees for the private school were too great a burden for my mother, who had just started working at a wedding hall. Although my father's salary as a judge had been fairly good, he did not leave anything that could be called an inheritance. I was only in the middle of my first term at school when he died, and not feeling any strong connection to that particular school, I was surprised by my mother's apology for the change and felt it was unnecessary.

When I actually started, however, I found it very difficult. The children in the class rushed about with whoops of glee; the teacher, dressed in sweatpants, shouted. Everything was drastically different from the girls' school. I could not help feeling that it was too late for me to make friends in the middle of such a boisterous clamor. But these were not the only reasons I found it hard.

As soon as I went back, I began to think. Where, I asked myself, did my father go? One day, he simply vanished. What did that mean? How could one cease, so suddenly, to exist? My father had virtually disappeared, like some cartoon character with his head in the clouds falling down an open manhole.

Of course, I was present at his funeral, and even when I looked into the coffin and saw his face, clearly not the same as when he was alive, I felt no fear. Yet that did not mean I understood his death. Where on earth did he go?

During the summer, when it was just my mother and I, or even when I was on my own, I never thought about this. Maybe I was not yet at the stage where I *could* think about it. But as soon as I stepped out into the world again, I had the strongest feeling that it was full of open manholes. My mother, and even I myself, could, at any time, fall into one of those dark holes, never to return. Like my father. The other children and the teacher at school appeared so bright and cheerful and strong. I could not believe any of them were aware of the existence of these dreadful holes. I felt terribly alone. There was no one in whom I could confide my fears, not even my mother.

She still avoided talking about my father, and even a child like myself could sense her strong rejection of his death. Not long after, I was to grow impatient with her stubborn denial, becoming angry and even critical of her, but at that time all I knew was that I must not mention my father to her. Besides, she was obviously suffering, and she did not find working easy. She had married my father, many years her senior, immediately after she graduated from a women's college, and having stayed at home even during the long period before I was born, she had hardly any work experience at all. I could not cause her more worry, not when I saw her, usually so calm and placid about everything, staying up late every night taking notes, a harassed expression on her face.

When she asked me, "How's school? Did you make any friends yet?" I'd answer, "Yeah. It's fun." Then when morning came, I would grit my teeth and head off into a world full of bottomless manholes with black, yawning maws that God might have forgotten to close. Although I did my homework conscientiously, and never forgot anything, all I can recall from that period is being constantly nervous that I might make a mistake. I was convinced that not making mistakes was the only way to avoid being sucked into those dark holes that might appear anywhere, anytime.

My anxiety increased with each passing day. I checked my schoolbag every night three times before I went to bed, and could not feel secure until I had checked it again before I left the house in the morning. I began to fear that the class schedule might change overnight, catching me unprepared, so I packed all my books and notebooks in my backpack each evening, and those that would not fit I put in a shoulder bag. My back was stooped under the heavy load, and I must have looked like an old miser woman as I trudged to and from school every day.

But the price of anxiety is fixed. When you nip one worry in the bud, another one will sprout up in its stead. So when I had virtually eliminated the possibility of forgetting something, I was beset by another worry. My mother left for work before I went to school, leaving me responsible for locking the door behind me. Now, however, I would make it halfway to school and suddenly be seized with doubt. Had I really locked the door?

Like Jack's beanstalk, this new worry grew at a phenomenal rate. In less than a week, I could no longer make it to school without going through a special ritual. Despite my heavy load, I would return home to check the lock precisely three times, turning back in a different spot each time. And of course, not once was the door unlocked. Nor did I ever find our house burned to the ground. It was just that if I did not return to check, I would be tormented by the fear that something terrible would happen.

In the case of the door, all I had to do was check that it was locked. My next worry, then, was being late for school. I only lived a ten-minute walk away, but because I was now lugging such an enormous load and had to retrace my steps three times, I could not be sure of getting to school on time without leaving an hour earlier. I believed that if I slept in, something awful would happen.

Once I finally reached school, my next concern was for my mother's safety. Would she be killed in a traffic accident like my father? Would she fall ill from exhaustion? Perhaps, even now, at that very moment, she was calling out to me for help.

The worst time of all was at night. When I lay in bed

and closed my eyes, dark, gaping manholes snapped open and shut, taunting me: "While you slumber, all that you hold dear is ours for the taking."

I pretended to sleep, waiting for my mother to come to bed. Only when I heard the sure sound of her peaceful breathing could I finally fall into oblivion myself, all the while invoking the aid of heaven to save me from sleeping in.

Strangely enough, I have no memory of *higan*, the autumnal equinox when special Buddhist services are performed for the dead. It was the first equinox after my father's funeral, so we must have done something, but I seem to have been so fanatically absorbed in my own rituals that all other memories were banished from my mind.

Then one morning in early October I came down with a fever, something that might have been expected.

"If your temperature doesn't go down this afternoon, we'll go see the doctor, all right?"

"But, Mom, don't you have to work?"

"Don't worry. One day off won't hurt."

For the first time in a long while, I actually rested. Any guilty feelings I might have had about making my mother take time off work were tempered by my fever. All I needed to do was sleep quietly, slip the thermometer under my armpit when my mother told me to, and let her feed me grated apple from a spoon that felt cool to my tongue. I'd sleep, and when I opened my eyes, my mother would be there at the table reading a book from work about the intricate customs of the Japanese wedding ceremony. As soon as she noticed that my eyes were open, she would get up and change the wet cloth on my forehead. When I had to go to the bathroom, she would slip a cardigan around my shoulders and wait, watching the door until I had finished.

I was extremely thankful for my fever. I wouldn't even mind getting worse, I thought, if it meant such peace of mind, such warmth and comfort.

"Mom?"

"What?"

"Nothing. I just wanted to call you, that's all."

I think I must have been sleeping quite deeply for some time when an indistinct noise began to cloud the limpid silence of my slumber. It sounded like an animal growling.

Startled awake, I realized that it was the sound of our washing machine, which was situated just outside our front door. My mother was asleep at the table, her forehead resting on the open book. I sat up, wondering when she had started doing the laundry. I hadn't even noticed. I looked at the clock; it was almost noon. I had slept so well that my body felt light and refreshed, and I rose and tiptoed to the entranceway.

I opened the door on a young man, a complete stranger, who was standing in front of our washing machine. He looked just as surprised as I was, and practically tumbled down the stairs in his haste to escape. Stepping out onto the balcony in my bare feet, I felt my heart begin to pound and I screamed. My mother came rushing out of the apartment, and almost simultaneously Mr. Nishioka, dressed in a sweat suit, burst out of the door next to ours. The smell of sleep and the low murmur of *rakugo*, a traditional Japanese form of comic storytelling, seeped slowly out of his room.

Although Mr. Nishioka was an introverted man who never joked, he must have played such comedy tapes all the time because we often heard the sound of a man's voice rising and falling in a continuous monologue through the wall of our apartment. Maybe he left the tape recorder running even when he was asleep.

That day he had just come off the night shift, and he looked ghastly, as if he had just woken up. His eyelids were swollen, and his normally messy hair was even more disheveled than usual. He grew his hair long on one side, and it now hung down like limp seaweed, exposing his drastically receding hairline to plain view. Startled by the appearance of this scrawny man looking like a fugitive in his fluff-covered sweat suit, I gave another high-pitched scream.

"Chiaki, what's wrong? Are you all right?" My mother shook me, but all I could do was point to the stairs. The figure of a man like the one I had just seen flashed by along the road beside the river. Mr. Nishioka, without any further knowledge of the circumstances, dashed down the stairs, as if someone had yelled, "Go!" My mother and I stood for some time gazing in confusion at laundry we did not recognize—men's underpants, socks, gym clothes— revolving round and round in our washing machine.

"Mom?"

"Yes."

"Was that guy doing his laundry here?"

"Looks like it."

"Doesn't he have a washing machine?"

"I guess not."

"What are we going to do with this stuff?"

"Hmmm."

My mother was still thinking when the washing machine stopped. Fearfully, I pressed the button to let the water drain out. With a loud "thunk," the murky gray water began to flow out the drainpipe. My mother brought a large plastic bag from the kitchen and with a grimace began throwing the soapy laundry into the bag. Mr. Nishioka, puffing with exertion, returned, saying, "Wha-what a despicable creature. Is he too stingy to use the coin-operated laundry?" His eyes were fixed on the bulging bag, his eyebrows, always very mobile, raised and quivering. He stood there fidgeting and muttering repeatedly in a rather high girlish voice, "Despicable, despicable."

Peering out from behind my mother, I said "Hello," and he bobbed his head in greeting just as he would to an adult. "Uh, I'm sorry. He got away," he said, and then he brushed the long hair that was dangling down the left side of his face over the top of his head, as if he had only just noticed.

My mother told me to go back to bed, and I returned to our room. But I left the door open so that I could hear what they were saying.

"You know, it's possible, it's just possible, that this might not have been the first time," Mr. Nishioka said. I started.

"No, really!" my mother protested in a nervous voice.

"Yes, it's possible. The landlady lives alone on the first floor, and n-nobody in the ap-apartments is home during the day." At high speed and with an occasional stutter, he explained that although he worked nights and was technically there during the day, he was usually sound asleep. That day he had just happened to get up to go to the toilet.

They decided to put the bagful of laundry out with the garbage in the morning when it would be collected, but until then my mother insisted on leaving it outside the gate in case he came back for it. She did not want to invite unnecessary hostility. The two picked up the bag and carried it downstairs. As I lay in bed and listened to their footsteps, I thought to myself with childish seriousness, It is all my fault. I'm being punished for staying home from school and making Mother take time off work. I even thought I wouldn't mind getting sicker. If I had gone to school, my mother would have gone to work and nobody would have used our washing machine. Everything would have worked out fine.

I shut my eyes tightly. A manhole cover opened with a clang and a voice from the depths of the earth grated unpleasantly in my ears: "Your greatest enemy is carelessness. Never forget."

Right, I told myself. I mustn't stay home from school tomorrow. I can't afford to relax my guard against those dark holes even for a moment. And I shut my eyes firmly once again.

## Chapter 3

UT THE MORE I TRIED, the more my body refused to listen. Although it was never very high, my temperature kept rising and falling and my mother had already taken a whole week off work on my behalf. During that period, I dreamed that I was pursued by moving manholes, and whenever I awoke, I would sit up groggily and attempt to dress for school, leaning my throbbing head against the dresser. Sometimes I would even start changing in the middle of the night. Let's see, I would think, my textbooks and notebooks are still packed in my knapsack and shoulder bag as they should be. Pencils sharpened? Yes. Eraser? Yes. Gym clothes? Yes. Lunch apron? Yes. Harmonica? Yes. Colored pencils? Yes.

Then the doctor made his awful pronouncement. "I

think your daughter should be admitted to the hospital for a while." At the word "hospital," I shook my head vehemently. I would never agree to being thrown into yet another unknown environment.

"But, Chiaki, if you go into the hospital, you'll be able to go back to school again soon," my mother pleaded, looking distressed.

"That's a lie."

"No, it's not."

"I don't need to go to the hospital. I'm going to go back to school tomorrow." I stubbornly insisted that I would rather go to school than be hospitalized. The doctor finally decided that if I was so adamant it would be better to take care of me at home. My mother, however, was in a dilemma because if she took any more time off, she risked losing her job. Just as she was wondering what on earth to do, the landlady volunteered to look after me.

"As your landlady, I must accept some responsibility for this. While you're at work, I'll take care of Chiaki." She seemed to have concluded that my nervous condition was due to the washing machine incident, and she felt very bad about it. She insisted that she should never have left the gate to Poplar House open.

"Chiaki, when I go to work every morning, you are to go to the landlady's. She's offered to spread a futon out for you so that you can rest." My mother's words came as a tremendous shock. Was she telling me to sleep in that weird room we'd seen? It was obvious that the landlady did not like children because in the beginning she had said, "No children allowed." Why, this was just as bad as sending me to stay with a wicked witch!

"Can't she come up to our room?"

"She's been having trouble with her knees recently, and she says it's hard for her to climb the stairs. And if you sleep there, she won't have to worry about you." My mother laughed and poked my cheek with her finger. "It's just during the day, you know."

"I can stay at home by myself. I'll be good."

"I'll stop by as soon as I get back from work and we can come home together. Don't be stubborn. Please." There was nothing I could say to that. And besides, if I didn't go, the landlady was sure to feel insulted.

The next day I left "for work" with my mother. The landlady had prepared a futon for me in the weird room, which adjoined a wood-floored kitchen. It appeared to be a sort of living room. Perhaps "living room" is a rather odd description, but this is where the landlady always sat, sipping green tea while reading the newspaper or watching television, her legs tucked into the *kotatsu*, a low, heated table with a quilt on top. So, although the room was carpeted rather than covered in traditional woven tatami, I was sure that it must classify as a living room. But as we had seen when we peered down the corridor from the entranceway on that first day, it was rather spooky for a living room. There was a built-in bookcase stacked to the ceiling with old books, and the room was full of strange ornaments, such as a dragon carved from green stone and a wall hanging with oddly shaped characters that looked like the wispy hairs of a wraith. Beside the sliding glass door that opened onto the garden stood an imposing chest of drawers, pitch black, with golden metal handles, and a futon was on the floor right up against it. I lay down on the futon with my back to the dresser, only to find myself staring into the eyes of an old man in a faded photograph that stood in a frame on the Buddhist altar. There was not a single hair on his head, yet his white beard almost covered his chest, and although his face looked rather timid, this did not make him any less daunting a companion. To my relief, the landlady had at least opened all the shutters, either out of consideration for me or simply due to the change in the season.

Every morning I ran a comb through my short hair, put on my best pajamas with the strawberry pattern and a blue cardigan of heavy wool, and went to the landlady's. After bidding her good morning, I crawled under the heavy cotton-stuffed quilt on the futon. The first two or three days I was too nervous to sleep. I lay there listening to the ticktock of the clock, unable even to drowse, while the landlady, either because she thought I was sleeping or because she did not care, spoke to me only when it was time to take my temperature or drink my medicine.

But I could not get away with just lying there the entire day. At noon, I got up to eat the two rice balls my mother had prepared for me. The landlady's lunch menu was invariably the same: cold rice, kelp stewed in soy sauce, and miso soup with turnip in it. She always served me some of the soup, but my mother never put turnip in our miso soup, and the landlady's was so repulsive it convinced me that only she herself could make it. She boiled it until the turnip was almost sludge, and the broth was so salty it made me desperate with thirst every time I drank it.

The landlady, oblivious of my aversion, always slurped it right down to the last drop, retrieving with infinite care any remaining turnip leaves from the bowl with her chopsticks and popping them in her mouth. Despite having only three teeth, all of them on the bottom, she munched her way through everything from pickles to rock-hard crackers. I often found myself riveted by her face, watching her eat. But just when I felt that my very soul was about to be sucked into her cavernous mouth, she would give me a sharp glance and say, "My, my, aren't you a slowpoke." Then I would hastily raise my bowl, for if she told my mother that I had no appetite, the day of my release from this purgatory would be further postponed.

Even worse than the soup, the landlady made me drink *senjicha*, a strongly steeped medicinal tea. The flavor was indescribable, both bitter and sour at the same time, and she drank it every day, "to improve my circulation." The first day she made me drink it, I knew instantly that this concoction was the source of the peculiar smell that pervaded her house. "If you want to get better, you had better drink it. Don't worry. You'll soon get used to it." With tears welling in my eyes, I gulped it down, desperately suppressing the urge to vomit. I will never ever, I thought with resignation, get used to this, not even if I grow as old as her.

I mutely endured those days of soup and *senjicha* and the massive quilt. I could think of nothing to talk about, and I believed, rather fatalistically, that it was better to remain silent than to speak and err. I wonder what the landlady thought. Perhaps it merely confirmed for her that she didn't like children.

I can still clearly remember when the landlady and I first had what could be called a proper conversation.

"I'm going to the eye doctor. I'll be back soon."

It was the first time she had gone out since I began staying with her. Although I didn't really like being left alone with her every day, suddenly I felt like saying, "Wait a minute! That wasn't the agreement." But because she announced her plans without the least trace of compunction, as if it was the most natural thing in the world, I could only nod dumbly, unable to utter a word.

I see, I told myself, she has things to do, too. I guess I must be the only person in the whole world who spends the day just sleeping and waking, or at the very most reading a book.

Feeling forlorn, I listened to the sounds she made as she bustled in and out of the room, changing her clothes, checking that she had turned off the gas.

She stepped out into a light rain. But later it began to pour and everything grew steadily darker. She had said that she would be back soon, but how long was soon? The more I worried about the time, the more the ticktocking of the wall clock fixed itself stubbornly in my brain. And when I glared at the clock, the drip-dripping of water falling from the drainpipe onto the ground outside got on my nerves so that I couldn't bear it. I felt like my fever must be rising, and I tossed and turned under the blankets. As I did so, I kept my eyes half-open, uncertain as to whether I should close them to shut out the sight of the things around me—the books with their bindings faded by the sun, the photo of the landlady's husband, the yellowed wall hanging, the bared fangs of the ornamental dragon— or keep a sharp watch on them.

I must have fallen asleep. When I opened my eyes with a start, it was so bright it seemed as if everything around me were shining like gold. I lay there dazed for a few moments. I glanced at the clock. It was past noon. About two hours had passed since the landlady left the house. And she had told me that she would be back soon! Of course I would not admit that I was actually waiting for her.

The earlier darkness had vanished like a dream. I rose from the futon and slid open the glass door that faced the garden.

For the first time in my life I really understood what it meant to be invigorated. I filled my lungs with the chilly autumn air, fresh from the rainfall, and saw that it was the poplar tree which caused everything around me to shine with gold.

Forgetting the cold, I gazed up at the enormous tree towering into the crystal sky. A transparent light was pouring through its yellow leaves. When did it change color? I wondered. I used to look at it every day during the summer. What had happened since then?

At that moment, the dog on the corner three houses down from Poplar House began to bark furiously. He was a useless dog that yapped at anyone. Obviously, someone must be passing his house. Sure enough, looking toward the hedge, I glimpsed a green umbrella bobbing nearer. Someone was slowly coming this way, umbrella open despite the fact that the rain had ceased. It was the landlady.

She swayed from right to left with each step, perhaps because her back was so stooped. The purse hanging from her elbow swayed, too, appearing and disappearing behind the hedge.

Suddenly, a bird slightly smaller than a pigeon burst from between the leaves of the poplar with a piercing cry, and the landlady stopped. She stretched her neck out like a turtle and peered up at the sky, resting the umbrella on her hunched back.

She looks just like Popeye, I thought. But her face was less villainous than usual.

When she caught sight of me standing on the narrow ledge outside the sliding door, she appeared slightly taken aback. The fresh air was bracing, and it put me in good spirits to have surprised her. She was always so imperturbable and never deigned to use a gentle, coaxing tone with children.

I announced in a loud, slightly hoarse voice, "It has stopped raining, you know." But she just smiled, her mouth becoming a single large wrinkle almost completely buried under her nose. She made no attempt to close her umbrella.

I thrust my feet into the wooden sandals, still damp with rain, which she kept beneath the ledge, and walked through the garden to the gate. It squeaked every time it moved, but even so she had kept it closed since the washing machine incident.

I opened it for her and tried again. "It's not raining anymore."

"I know." Then, following the direction of my gaze as I stood there gaping, she added, "I'm drying it."

"Huh?"

"You should always dry your umbrella after you've used it in the rain. Didn't you know?"

Her matter-of-fact tone implied that it was perfectly normal to dry one's umbrella while walking down the street, and all I could say was, "Sure, I know that."

"Hurry along inside. You shouldn't be out here dressed like that," she said, already heading for the sliding glass door. Leaving her umbrella, still wet, on the stone step, she heaved herself through the doorway, grunting with the effort, and disappeared inside the house. She did not forget to take her shoes with her to place them neatly in the front entranceway. Left standing there, I sneezed.

That was the first memorable conversation I ever had with her. Not long after that, I caught her with her umbrella open on a sunny day. When I pointed out that it was already dry, she brushed me off by claiming that she was using it as a parasol.

"Do you like turnip in your miso soup?" I asked her one day.

"Yes, I do."

"Why?"

"Why? Because I do. You don't have to have a reason for liking or not liking something, you know."

Although as usual she did not speak to me very much, she did answer, if somewhat brusquely, when I asked a question. A typical conversation might go something like:

"How old are you, Mrs. Yanagi?"

"Hmm. I wonder."

But there were times when she said more. One day I noticed that she had a bald spot on the back of her head. Her hair was pure white without a trace of yellowing, and it had a slight wave to it that gave it body. It was cut in a short bob slicked down in the back. When she was thinking about something, she had a habit of placing the palm of her hand against the top of her head slightly toward the back. Between the white hairs in this area I glimpsed her scalp, so shiny and smooth that I could not believe it was part of the same skin that covered her deeply wrinkled, weathered face.

"Do girls go bald, too?" I asked in the most tactful way I could. But although I was sure she would never guess that I was thinking of her, she immediately said, "Oh, you mean this," and touched her hair. I was mortified, but she did not seem to mind.

"I was very fastidious when I was young. Everything had to be done just right. When I put my hair up in a bun

I used to pull it so tightly that it stretched the skin on my face. That's why I have this."

"What's a bun?"

"A bun is a bun. It's the way people used to do their hair in the old days."

"Like the samurai movies on TV?"

"That's a bit further in the past than I was thinking, but something like that."

"Did you wear a kimono, too?"

"Of course. Everyone used to wear them."

"So, if you tie your hair too tight, you'll go bald?"

"That's right. Better be careful."

"I will."

I think that as I started to direct my attention outward, I began to let the outside world in.

I enjoyed watching the poplar lose its leaves day by day. When I glimpsed a red fruit through its now sparser leaves, I became very excited.

"That's a snake gourd," the landlady told me. "The vine is wrapped around the tree. The birds will come and peck at it soon."

About the same time, I noticed that stray cats often visited her garden. They seemed to find it very cozy, crawling into the undergrowth of peonies and scrub iris, or lying on the edge of the blue porcelain brazier that had been placed in the middle of the yard. Along with the lunch my mother made me, I began taking a cup of milk to the land-lady's house. Although she grumbled that she hated cats because they pooped in her yard and scared the birds away, she gave me a cracked saucer into which I poured the milk, and I placed it by the laundry rack right beside the narrow ledge outside the sliding glass door.

One day my fever came back and the landlady pulled the futon out for me again to let me rest. I was sleeping when I heard her talking outside. "Don't you start that again. Stop it right now." I got up and opened the sliding door. Although it was a clear sunny day, the air was nippy. It must have been November already.

She was standing in the yard squinting up toward where the lack of leaves was becoming obvious, with four or five cats around her. In contrast to her, the cats were hunched over, eyes focused on the ground, and their mouths were moving energetically. The landlady raised her voice toward the sky once more. Her throat had slackened with age, and her voice broke into a high falsetto when she tried to shout. "Miss Sasaki. Stop that. I have told you time and again. I don't mind if you feed the cats, but please stop throwing food from up there. Come down and feed them in one place."

I leaned out of the doorway and looked up. I could see the pale face of Miss Sasaki, who looked as if she had just woken up, at the window of the west apartment.

Miss Sasaki worked for a company that made costumes

for plays and entertainment shows at amusement parks. She always wore slim-cut jeans, and she smoked cigarettes while she walked. I had never seen her wear makeup. Although she was almost the same age as my mother, she seemed more like a university student.

Once when I was putting the saucer of milk for the cats out by the laundry rack, she had spoken to me. "You must be the little Hoshino." I nodded without saying anything. "How old are you?" I showed her six fingers. I thought that she might comment on my rather babyish behavior, but she paid no attention to it and instead crouched down beside me, saying abruptly, "I have a question for you. Are you trying to copy my hairstyle?"

We did indeed have the same short pageboy cut. I remained still as stone, unable even to shake my head, certain that she was disgusted to find that a child like me had the same haircut. But then she said, "Hey, come on. I was only trying to point out that we have something in common. I guess you don't understand a joke when you hear one." And with that she exhaled a stream of smoke, stood, and walked slowly up the stairs.

The landlady raised her voice again. She seemed to be quite annoyed. "Miss Sasaki, do you understand me? When you feed the cats, please put the food—"

"Soorrry!" Miss Sasaki pulled her head in and closed the window in a leisurely fashion.

Looking more carefully around the yard from my position on the ledge, I noticed the end of a fish-paste sausage lying on the ground. The heftiest-looking tomcat sidled over to it and swiftly clamped it in his jaws. The rest of the cats continued gazing upward as if waiting for manna to fall from heaven. "Too bad for you, you pitiful beasts," the landlady grumbled as she took off her sandals. Then to me she said, "You'd better get back into bed or your fever will rise."

She seemed very irritable, so I quickly slid back under the quilt. Inside the covers it was cozy and warm, and I shivered at the sudden change.

"That Miss Sasaki. When she's out of sorts, she always does something odd." She continued muttering to herself even when she had settled down at the *kotatsu* again.

"When she's out of sorts, does she feed the cats from upstairs?" I asked, with just my eyes peeping over the top of the quilt.

"Who knows."

"But you just said that she did."

"Then I guess she does."

I thought for a minute. "You're wrong," I said.

The landlady looked at me in surprise. "How am I wrong?"

"I think she does it because it's fun."

"You mean she's making a game of it at her age? Balderdash."

The way she said "balderdash" struck me as hilarious and I giggled. She glared at me, her eyes gleaming. "And if you're thinking of trying it yourself, don't bother."

Of course, Miss Sasaki continued to scatter manna from above, driving the landlady mad, and although I know it was rather unkind, I found this very amusing.

# Chapter 4

THE LANDLADY had a rapacious appetite for sweets and always bought a treat from the Nishikawa shop on her way home from the eye doctor. And that treat was always four *mamedaifuku*, a confection made with pounded sticky rice, studded with black beans, and stuffed with bean jam.

Of the four, the landlady invariably took out two and placed each on a separate plate. Giving one plate to me, she would carry the other to the Buddhist family altar. There she would strike a small bowl-shaped brass gong, fold her hands in prayer, and then immediately retrieve the sweet that she had just placed there as an offering and begin eating it.

"But there are still some left that you could use as offerings," I ventured to remark one day, eyeing the two remaining sweets in the plastic container.

"My Professor never liked sweets. Anyway, it's the thought that counts," she said indifferently, continuing to chew methodically. She called the man with the long white beard in the photograph on the altar her Professor.

By this time, I was much recovered, and had made a great deal of progress in my study of the landlady, so I knew the statement that he "never liked sweets" was a lie. She was just fanatically tidy.

Although she considered doing laundry to be troublesome and hated cooking so much that her body, already stooped, seemed to shrivel with annoyance just standing in the kitchen, when it came to tidying she was very quick. Be it a knife, nail clippers, a pen, or freshly dried laundry, if she was not using it right that instant, she put it away, even if she knew she'd be using it again five minutes later. And until she had tidied something away, her gaze was never still.

So I knew that she could not possibly bear to watch sweets placed on the altar dry out and collect dust. It was the same with the freshly cooked rice she placed there as an offering each morning—she struck the gong only once and then whisked the rice away and put it back in the rice cooker.

We had a brand-new family altar in our apartment upstairs. I couldn't help but feel that it, and even the photograph of my father that had been placed upon it, were unapproachable. Although at times she sat absently in front of it, my mother, like me, seemed to find it hard to accustom herself to an altar which, although it had all the trappings, had no substance. The fruit placed before it as an offering sat there for a long time.

"Why do you bother putting offerings on the altar?"

The landlady took one of the two remaining sweets, her second, from the plastic container.

"Help yourself to another one."

I shook my head. "Why do you?"

"Well, now . . ."

"Like fruit—even if you place it as an offering, it just goes rotten."

She tilted her head slightly.

"My mother, she never talks about my father. But she still puts offerings on the altar."

With my limited vocabulary, I struggled to explain my thoughts. The fact that the bananas we placed on the altar turned black just like ordinary bananas left on the table proved to me that we—mother and child—no longer had any connection with my father. If my father was really watching over me, as people who came to the funeral insisted, then why did he ignore our offerings?

"If he was really there, then something amazing ought to happen. Like the fruit suddenly vanishing, or never going bad—"

I stopped talking abruptly, struck by a sudden revelation. It's true, I thought. On that day, the day my father died, my mother and I, like the rotting fruit, were abandoned, powerless to do anything about it . . .

"Your father is watching over you," the landlady said.

"That's not true!" I responded, suddenly obdurate. "You never even met him."

"I don't need to have met him to know that he is watching over you."

"How can you know that when you've never been dead?"

"I don't have to have died. I am already closer to the grave than you are."

"Well, then, why aren't you dead yet?"

"That is the one thing over which we have no control." Despite my belligerence, she remained unperturbed. "After all, I'm not a ghost, so I will certainly die someday."

"But when is someday?"

"Ah, that's the question." She resettled herself on the cushion, giving me her usual one-wrinkle smile. "It doesn't matter when I die. But I have a job to do."

"A job?"

"That's right."

I immediately forgot my frustration. "What job?"

"Can you keep a secret?"

"Yes."

"If you can, then I'll tell you." She licked the tip of her finger and with it began collecting the white specks of flour that had fallen from the sweet onto her skirt.

"But first would you bring in the laundry for me?"

Clearing her scrawny throat, she sipped some tea.

🌱

When the landlady told me that her job was to deliver letters, a vision of her riding astride a sturdy red motor scooter flashed across my mind.

"You're a mailman?"

She hunched over in her seat and chuckled. "Hee, hee, hee. To the next world, yes."

"Huh?"

"I deliver mail to the next world. When it is my turn to go, I will carry letters from this world." She took a tissue and began pushing it up one of her nostrils. "It hasn't rained much lately," she remarked. I dragged the wastebasket closer and placed it within reach. I hated being asked to throw away her tissues with dried-up clumps of snot in them.

"If you can have a letter delivered, it's different from just thinking that you are connected to someone in the next world, you know, even if you believe it from the bottom of your heart."

"Why?"

"Because the letter really gets there."

I found it difficult to grasp what she was saying. In my mind, I could still see her riding around on a red mail scooter with a white paper triangle on her forehead, like those put on the corpse at a funeral, and her toothless mouth open, laughing.

"When my grandmother died," she began, rolling her tissue into a little ball and dropping it into the wastebasket, "I said to her as she lay in her coffin, 'Please take this letter to my cousin Kosuke for me.'"

"You put the letter in her coffin?"

"Yes, that's right."

"Was your grandmother really old?"

"Yes. Really old. But I think that she was probably younger than I am now."

"Were you a child?"

"Yes, a child. I was just nine years old."

I tried to imagine her carrying a schoolbag, but my mind went blank.

"Kosuke was quite a bit older, but he often played with me. He was very kind."

"Did he die? Was he sick?"

She nodded. "That was a year for funerals. First my uncle, from the main branch of the family, fell in the river, then Kosuke caught a cold that worsened, and finally my grandmother . . ."

"What did you write in your letter?"

"I asked him to come and see me again."

I caught my breath. I remembered a comic book I had read in the dentist's office. I think it was a famous story rewritten for children. It was about a couple who lost their son in the war and found a mummified monkey's hand that would grant them three wishes. One stormy night their dead son returned from the grave, with two hollow cavities for eyes, and rotting flesh beneath his tattered clothing . . .

"Did he come back from the dead?" I whispered hoarsely, but the landlady glanced at the last remaining sweet as if to say, "There's no rush."

"Are you sure you don't want this?" she said.

"Yes. Go ahead. You eat it."

"All right, then. Why don't you pour me another cup of tea?"

She drank the tea I clumsily poured for her and devoured her third sweet. Following that, she cleared her throat repeatedly, and when she had finished, blew her nose, combed her hair with her fingers, and asked me to pour her yet another cup.

Then, just when I had reached the height of exasperation, she said, "This is the important part," and finally resumed her tale. "After my cousin Kosuke died, I began to walk in my sleep."

"You walked while you were sleeping?"

"Yes."

"You're kidding!"

"No, I'm not. In the morning my feet and bedclothes were covered with mud. Nobody understood what was happening. My mother once tied my leg to hers with a cloth cord, but not wanting to hurt me, she tied it too loosely and it came undone, and I was off, wandering all over. It's very odd, but even though I was walking in my sleep I never fell off a high place or was injured in any way." She nodded to herself. "It's a mental disturbance called somnambulism, you know."

"You mean you were sick?"

"Yes, I was." She seemed almost proud of it.

"Because you were sad that your cousin had died?"

"Yes, I was sad, certainly. But not just sad—somehow I was frightened. Because someone with whom I used to play every day, someone with whom I had shared meals, was suddenly gone." Her eyes were closed. Without realizing it, I nodded at her words, and as if she had seen me, she said, "You understand."

"Yes."

But in the next instant, she veered off in a completely different direction from mine. "He was my first love, you see."

She blinked her eyes like a cat napping in the sun and then made a sound through her nostrils: "Hnn, hnn, hoo."

I could not distinguish whether it was a mere snort or actual laughter.

Having no interest in the story of her first love, I plowed on. "And did you get better?"

She started out of her reverie and slapped her knees, announcing, "That's just it! As soon as my dead grandmother took my letter, my somnambulism ceased, just like that."

"Really?"

"Kosuke must have read it and healed me, don't you think? After all, I wrote that I was sick, too."

"Do you really think so?"

"Of course. Because that's not all. I did meet him again."

We were finally getting to the heart of the story, and I leaned forward. Then she really did meet a zombie in the graveyard, I thought. And it was the horror of that experience which did this to her face . . .

She pointed, gesturing slowly with her extended arm. Fearfully I followed the direction of her finger to the bearded old man in the black-and-white photograph. His eyes were small and timid, as usual.

"When I first met my Professor."

"Yes?" I held my breath.

"I was amazed. He looked exactly like Kosuke. It was Kosuke who brought me and my Professor together."

"They looked alike?"

"That's right."

"How alike?"

"How alike? Like a living replica. His face, his physique, the shape of his fingernails. And here on his neck . . ." She raised her chin and grasped the wrinkled skin on her own neck. The color, shape, and size were just like the triangular head of a dried squid. "Right here, they both had a mole."

"Hmmm." So it wasn't a zombie after all, I thought, somewhat disappointed, but I looked once more at the old man's photograph.

"Was your cousin bald?"

"No, silly! When he was young, my Professor had plenty of hair."

"Oh."

"Although he did start to go bald rather early . . ."

She rose with a grunt and, seating herself in front of the altar, struck the gong and began to pray. Although it seemed like we were praying for the repose of her Professor's deceased hair, I also folded my hands together.

"Anyway"—the landlady turned to face me again—"I was very glad that my grandmother had taken my letter for me."

"When your husband died, did he take a letter to Kosuke for you, too?"

"No."

"Why not?"

"Obviously, because he would have been jealous. Besides"—she got up stiffly and returned to settle herself down on the cushion—"when he died, I thought about it, you know. I thought, I no longer need someone to deliver letters for me. It's my turn to take the letters for someone else. That's the job I was talking about before."

I see, I thought, impressed. I did not understand everything, but her words were convincing.

"At my age, they could be coming to take my soul at any moment. Now is the time to earn my wages."

"Wages? You mean you get paid for it?"

Her nostrils flared indignantly, as if demanding to know just what was wrong with that. "When you mail a letter, you put a stamp on it, right? Stamps are not free, you know."

"Yes, I know that, but . . ."

Seeing that I was not satisfied, she pointed to the black chest of drawers with golden handles that I always slept beside.

"The top drawer there. It's stuffed."

"Stuffed?"

"Stuffed." She nodded solemnly.

My eyes were riveted on the drawer. The landlady's

hoard of cash! But stuffed full? Incredible. The drawer could easily have accommodated ten sweaters.

"My mother—she always puts the money I get as New Year's gifts into my savings account," I remarked.

"You are a silly girl. Letters! It's stuffed with letters. In the twenty years since my Professor died, I've acquired quite a clientele."

"Can I look?"

"Certainly. But if you do, it'll be you who must take them to the next world."

Horrified, I hastily averted my eyes from the drawer. "What kind of people ask you?"

She stuck her neck out and fixed her slightly clouded yet very lively eyes on me. "Now listen carefully. I will not die until that drawer becomes so packed that you can't fit even one more letter inside. In other words, I will die when it is full. So I can't accept letters from just anybody. For example . . . " She lowered her voice. "That mailman who was here a while ago."

"I didn't see his face."

"He wasn't delivering. He came to give me a letter to take for him. Because his wife drowned in the bath."

"And?"

"I can't tell you any more. The names of my clients are confidential."

Not only her mouth but her eyes snapped shut as well,

and she hunched over even more than usual, looking like an old-fashioned figurine.

Suddenly I found myself asking, "How much does it cost?"

The slight wriggle of her nostrils did not escape my notice. But she said indifferently, "Well, that depends on the case. A letter to someone who died a long time ago is expensive."

"Why?"

"It's not going to be easy to find them over there, is it?"

How could she know that when she had never died herself?

"But if it's for someone who died recently, I can make it cheaper for you. After all, my grandmother did it for me for free a long time ago."

"Then do it for free. I'll write a letter."

"And just why should I do it for you for free? I can't agree to that."

"Because if you don't, I'll tell. Everyone."

She looked at my face as if to say, Oho, I see.

Inwardly I was shocked by my own words. Of course, I would write to my father, but until then it had never even occurred to me to do so, and I had no idea what to say. Frankly, I just wanted to demand that she do it for free. I don't think that it came from a desire for affection. It was more like a combative impulse.

"So you don't care if I tell?"

"Well, now."

"Then I'll tell."

"And I wonder whether anyone will take what you say seriously," she snorted, sipping her tea with unruffled calm. Her pug nose was almost completely flat between her eyes, with just its tip pointing upward.

Glaring at her, I suddenly felt angry and blurted out, "You liar."

"Oh? So you think I'm lying, do you?"

"That's right."

"Hmm." She gave me a sideways glance. "Then why don't you take a look in that drawer and see if I am or not?"

I fell silent abruptly.

"Well, how about it?"

"But . . . You said yourself it's a secret."

"It is."

"If it's a secret, then I shouldn't open it."

She said nothing but stood up, reached out her arms, and grasped the handles of the drawer, rattling them and muttering, "What have we here, now? Mm, it's heavy, it is." Her back was bent, and even without that she was short, so it was hard work for her to open the top drawer.

At that moment, I knew that her secret was safe. For if I looked inside the drawer, I would be the one to take the letters to the dead. Perhaps many people had already made that mistake and been forced to die in her stead. Was that the secret of her longevity?

"Eeyaah!" I could bear it no longer and covered my face with both hands, cowering on the floor.

The sound of the drawer sliding open reached my ears where I lay prostrate, my face hidden in the cushion. There was a rustling sound as of something being stirred, the landlady's ragged breathing, then I felt her drawing near, wafting a fragrance that reminded me of my mother's kimono, and heard the sound of paper crinkling right beside my ear.

"Won't you take a look? It's a brand-new one. Fresh."

Tears welled in my tightly shut eyes. She chuckled. "Come on. Open your eyes, just a little."

I pressed my face against the cushion so fiercely that I choked. Then I heard her walking away and the sound of the drawer closing.

"Well, well, look at that. Pulling your head in like a baby turtle. For someone who goes around calling others a liar, you ought to have more pride." But then, as I remained despondently silent, she suddenly said something quite unexpected. "For you, I'll do it for free. Bring me your letter."

"It's okay." I sat up and shook my head, thoroughly incensed. "I'm not going to write any dumb letter."

"Yes, I know."

"What?"

"I know. That's why I said that I'd do it for free."

She smiled a sly satisfied smile—the one that transformed her mouth into a single long wrinkle.

## Chapter 5

I STARTED GOING BACK TO SCHOOL on Monday of the following week. No longer afraid of forgetting things, or of thieves or fire, all I feared was those fears returning. Although I was not exactly elated about going to school, it seemed that I was learning, however little, to deal with the outside world.

When the girl who sat beside me in class remarked, "You know, I used to think you couldn't talk," I was shocked to realize how strange I must have appeared before, yet relieved, too, that she had told me so frankly. School gradually changed from a lawless wasteland full of open manholes into a world where words communicated.

Every day when school was over, I practically flew home to Poplar House to take my latest letter, written the previous night, to the landlady. Each time I handed her my envelope addressed "To Father, from Chiaki," she would rise heavily as if it were too much bother and, after warning me not to look, put the letter in the drawer. Not sure that closing my eyes was really sufficient, I pressed both hands firmly against them. Otherwise I was afraid that I might not be able to resist peeking. As I pressed against the thin skin covering my eyeballs, red and green blobs rose hazily against the blackness. They stayed hovering in the air about me for a few moments after I opened my eyes.

I wonder what I felt when I wrote those letters. At first, I don't think I had any strong desire to talk to my father, although it's true that deep inside somewhere I did feel the urge to write. The reality of my father's death, however, seemed unrelated to the letters that I addressed to him. I think instead that I simply enjoyed the landlady's reaction as she said, "What? You can write?" or "So you want me to die an early death, do you?"

My first letter went like this:

*Father,*
*How are you? I am fine.*
*Goodbye.*

The content of all my letters up to the fourth one was exactly the same. It would be correct to say that the fourth letter was different, not because I thought the rest had been just too pathetic, but because this time I actually had something to say.

> *Father,*
>
> *How are you? I turned seven today. Mother bought me a birthday cake. We cut it and I took a piece to the landlady. She calls cake Western sweets. I took some to our neighbors, Mr. Nishioka and Miss Sasaki, too. It was delicious. Mother bought me a book called* My Father's Dragon.
>
> *Goodbye.*

I was forced to sign off and shove the letter in an envelope at that point because my mother said, "Go to bed," but from the next day on I began writing about what was going on around me in a style appropriate to a seven-year-old. My letters were more like entries in a diary. With each passing day, I became more absorbed in this task. It felt amazingly good to be able to divulge everyday things to someone without worrying one bit about whether I was bothering him or about the possibility of being scolded.

By late November, the poplar tree was growing barer with each passing day, and five snake gourds hung from it, red and ripe. After school I would help the landlady sweep up the leaves. The bamboo broom was taller than I, and I suspect that it looked more as if the broom were pushing me. But I was a hard worker. When the landlady said, "All the leaves this tree sheds are a nuisance to the neighbors," I swept not only the yard but the entire street down to the house on the corner with the yappy dog. Although I knew very well that by the next day I would just have to sweep all over again, I was addicted to this very repetition. The skin between my index finger and thumb was rubbed raw many times where I gripped the broom. The landlady would dab it with medicine that stung terribly, saying each time, "You're so delicate." And she would chortle happily, comparing the contortions of my face with the extent of my injury.

A long time ago, when the landlady's husband first planted the poplar seedling, before the hedge had grown up around the house, the surrounding land was mostly empty and full of weeds, with just a handful of cultivated fields, some rude shacks, and a few farmhouses. At first the landlady was disappointed because it resembled the place where they had both grown up. "I argued. 'We left the country to live in a place like this?' I said. But my Professor, he fell in love with it. He was so disappointed when houses began to spring up around us. And he was right, too. It was better before. You don't have to sweep up the leaves if there are only empty fields around, right?" And she snorted through her nose.

When our pile of leaves had grown into a mountain, we often lit a bonfire. Leaves alone don't catch fire very easily, so the landlady would pour some kerosene from a container in the shed into an old coffee cup with no handle. She would dip a rolled-up newspaper into it and then light the paper with a match. She made an impressive figure with the torch flaming in her hand and her back hunched over. She would sprinkle the remaining kerosene from the cup over the mound of leaves, set the pile on fire at several spots with the torch, and then wait motionless for a while. The flames seemed very shy at first, peeping out from their nest like timid wild creatures. Then suddenly, they shed their modesty and rose together into a strong, rhythmically breathing blaze. Each time that moment came, so cozy-looking yet unpredictable, I would be taken by surprise, and the landlady, as if a spell had been broken, would begin to walk about the fire again.

I often crouched down and watched with bated breath as a scrap of paper or a leaf writhed and changed its shape within the flames. The bonfire reminded me of when I had seen my father's bones at the crematorium, and as the sight had not alarmed me, I began to think about his bones every time we burned the leaves, rerunning the memory over and over again in my mind until my father's bones gradually became divorced from other memories and simply remained a close and familiar thought.

If it happened that Miss Sasaki was at home, she would invariably be attracted by the smell of smoke and, leaping on her bicycle, would announce as she pedaled off, "I'll go buy some sweet potatoes." Following the landlady's directions, we wrapped the sweet potatoes in damp newspaper and then in tinfoil and slowly baked them in the fire. When eaten by the bonfire in the early twilight of a winter evening, with faces glowing from the heat of the flames and bodies stiff with cold, the piping-hot potatoes surpassed the most sumptuous meal.

If anyone chanced to pass by on the street, even if he was a complete stranger, Miss Sasaki would call out, "Would you like some baked sweet potato?" It intrigued me that the stronger the fire burned, the more easily people responded to the invitation. It might be a man out walking his dog, a woman selling insurance, or a boy pushing his bicycle, his face smeared with dirt and tears. I don't remember that we talked much. Perhaps we couldn't with our mouths full of hot sweet potato. But that memory—complete strangers gathered around the bonfire in the landlady's yard sharing food—is imprinted on my mind, a tranquil picture.

One day, I was waiting for the landlady in her yard. I supposed that she had gone to the eye doctor. I had been waiting for a long time after returning from school. The poplar was now almost completely bare, having been shaken every night by the north wind. As I swept up the yellow leaves, I thought to myself, When all the leaves are gone, we won't be able to have bonfires anymore. For the first time I realized that my job of sweeping leaves, which had seemed so perpetual, might one day end. Feeling somewhat bereft, I gripped the handle of the bamboo broom. When I had gathered the leaves into a pile, I squatted down to wait for the landlady, for, of course, I was not allowed to light a fire on my own. Although the wind had stopped, it was a cold, gray day. I gradually began to lose sensation in my bent legs and I could feel my body temperature slowly drop and falter.

"Hey! Hey!"

I heard a voice calling from afar and opened my eyes. I had fallen asleep while crouched on the ground. The marks of my teeth showed on my knees and my legs were tingling with numbness. Twilight had set in.

"Were you asleep?"

Startled, I looked up and saw the head of an enormous rabbit in front of me. The rabbit was wearing jeans and waved at me as I gazed up from my crouching position. "Miss Sasaki?"

"Mm. You could tell right away, could you?" She raised the rabbit head high and appeared from underneath. For a moment her hair floated upward with the rabbit's head and I thought, She's beautiful.

"We made this at my company. They said they don't need it anymore, so"—she thrust the giant rabbit's head toward me—"I thought you might like it."

I stood up unsteadily on my numb legs and tried it on. "I can't see anything. And it smells." I floundered in the pitch darkness.

"It won't work, then. The eyeholes are made for adults." She pulled it off my head. "Next time I'll bring you a child-size one," she said. I did not really have any desire to transform myself into a rabbit, but I thanked her just the same.

"Where's the old battle-ax?" Sometimes she called the landlady that.

"She's not here."

"Did she go out somewhere?"

"I think she's gone to the eye doctor."

"Hmm. Her eyes are bad, are they?"

"She says the doctor pulls out her eyelashes for her." I told her verbatim what the landlady had once told me. As she grew older, her eyelashes had begun to turn inward, and if she didn't get them pulled regularly, they would scratch her eyeballs.

"Must be because the skin on her eyelids has gotten flabby," Miss Sasaki said. She pressed her fingertips against her temples and pulled her eyes up like a fox's. After that we ran out of things to say to each other.

A darkness peculiar to this season with its short

days spread around us like black ink. "It's getting late," Miss Sasaki muttered to herself. "And I bought sweet potatoes."

I suddenly became anxious. If the landlady had gone to the eye doctor, then she was much too long coming back, and she had never in all the time I had been here returned home this late before. Maybe, yes, maybe the reason she had not come home yet . . .

"Miss Sasaki, remember you said that cats go away and hide when they know they are going to die?"

"Uh-huh."

"We'd better start looking for her."

"What?"

"She said that she would die. Once the drawer became full."

"Drawer? What drawer?"

How could I have been so stupid? Every day I had been bringing her letters, but it had never occurred to me that the drawer might fill up so fast.

"What's wrong? Get ahold of yourself."

Perhaps her voice reached Mr. Nishioka's room upstairs, because the window of the center apartment rattled open. The sound of laughter from a comedy show floated out into the night and I regained some sense of reality. "What's wrong?" Mr. Nishioka, dressed in a short, quilted dressing gown, leaned out from the window.

"It's Chiaki. She's worried because the landlady hasn't come back yet."

Annoyed that she was behaving as if I was the problem rather than showing any concern for the landlady, I said, "She might be dead." Although I could not see his face with the light from his room behind him, he seemed to be startled by my words. In a moment we heard his footsteps on the stairs, and he came into the yard, smoothing the long hank of hair on the left side across his thinning pate.

"Chiaki, why do you think she might be dead?" He shot the words out with his usual rapidity. I didn't want to say anything about the letters, but I felt somehow responsible because I had given her so many.

"Because she's so late," was all I said, but as soon as the words left my mouth I thought, I've become a liar, and to my surprise, large teardrops fell from my eyes and rolled down my cheeks.

The effect of my tears was impressive. Mr. Nishioka was thrown into such confusion that I felt guilty. He bobbed from one foot to the other. Miss Sasaki sighed and plunked the rabbit's head over me. "At any rate, we'd best start looking for her," Mr. Nishioka said in a rush. "Ch-ch-children's hunches are often right." Trapped within the smelly darkness of the rabbit head, I trembled when I heard his voice become shrill with apprehension. Oh no! I thought. My hunch might be right.

"Besides that, she might have gotten lost on her way home or something like that."

"Hardly," Miss Sasaki remarked wryly, her voice sounding as if she would like to have added, Not that old battle-ax.

"No, no. You never can tell. You never can tell. She might have been stricken with senility very suddenly."

"So?"

"Anyway, shouldn't we— Just a little?"

"And how do you suggest we go about looking for her?"

I was still struggling desperately to free myself from the rabbit head, finally falling over backward onto my bottom with a thump.

"I'm going to the eye doctor's," I announced when I had finally removed the odious thing from my head.

"Then I'll check the train station." Mr. Nishioka strode off purposefully, still wearing his dressing gown.

The eye clinic was already closed, and no matter how many times I rang the bell, nobody answered. Miss Sasaki and I walked along the streets, now completely dark, looking about in case the landlady had fallen somewhere. "I'm sure it's all right. She's probably already come home," said Miss Sasaki. She smoked a cigarette as she sauntered along.

My nostrils quivered. "Something smells good."

Miss Sasaki stopped for a second and sniffed the air. "Somebody's making curry somewhere."

The crisp, clean air of the first winter night, the smell of someone making curry, cigarette smoke. With a shock, I recognized that combination. I had encountered something like it once before. I was walking down the street with my father, just the two of us, with the smell of curry and my father smoking. The moon that night had been very big, a brilliant white full moon, I remembered, and I looked up at the sky.

"The moon!" I cried.

"Yeah, it's full," Miss Sasaki responded, breathing slow puffs of white steam.

"Do you really think the landlady might have come home?" I asked once more, and Miss Sasaki took my hand without a word and gripped it tightly.

When we returned to Poplar House, my mother was standing by the gate looking worried. She seemed a little surprised to see me with Miss Sasaki. "Mom, is the landlady back yet?" I asked.

"No. Is something wrong?"

Miss Sasaki explained the situation for me, as I was too disappointed. "It's partly my fault," she said. "I told Chiaki that cats go away to die, and it seems that has made her anxious."

My mother looked at me with some concern but then

said, "No. She's right. It's past seven already. It's quite reasonable to be worried." And she patted me lightly on the back as I drooped with discouragement.

"When she went on a seniors' trip to the hot spring, at least she warned me that she would be away." Miss Sasaki was becoming nervous herself, perhaps because it was after seven, and she kept peering toward the road by the river.

"Does she have any relatives?" my mother asked.

Miss Sasaki scratched her head doubtfully. "They didn't have any children. I heard once that she was his second wife." As the three of us stood by the gate wondering what to do, our breath frosting the air, Mr. Nishioka returned.

"No good. No good." He waved his arms exaggeratedly as though he had just accomplished some special mission on our behalf. "I waited at the ticket gate for a while, but then I realized it could take a long time, so I asked the man at the gate about her and came back home via the shopping arcade, stopping at the police station on the way." He suddenly noticed that my mother was with us and nodded his head, saying in as deep a voice as possible, "Hello."

"Why the police station?" Miss Sasaki demanded.

His eyebrows went into convulsions at this confrontation, and he said even more breathlessly than usual, "N-n-nothing, really. I j-just asked, that's all."

"And?"

"And? Well, I could hardly request them to begin a

manhunt. But anyway, they said that they had not heard of anyone like her being found."

Just then a black silhouette appeared from the road by the creek.

"Mrs. Yanagi."

The moonlight suddenly caught the landlady, as if in a spotlight. "My, my. Why are you all gathered here?" Her voice reached us, but I was immobilized by surprise and confusion.

She wore a black kimono like those worn for mourning. As she hardly ever wore kimonos, this was unusual in itself, but that was not what caught my attention. It was her face. When I had first met her, I suspected that the reason her face looked like an evil Popeye was because she had taken some strange potion, but now I was positive.

Her face, which was normally crumpled, had grown much longer. Looking closely, I realized that in fact it was just the lower half of her face which was elongated; her cheekbones were more defined and her wrinkles smoothed. It almost seemed as if she had grown younger. So that's it, I thought to myself. She's drunk a magic potion to bring back her youth. But she was lacking her usual liveliness that made it seem as though at any moment some evil genius might prompt her to do something mean. Even her voice had changed: it sounded muffled.

"My, I'm tired. Not much fun going to a wake, is it?

Here . . ." She opened her black handbag, took out her house key, and held it out to me. I approached her very timidly and took it. The entire time, my eyes were glued to her face.

"What are you staring at? Open the door for me," she said.

But the next instant I yelled, "Mrs. Yanagi has grown teeth!"

The landlady looked slightly put out and fell silent. Then she said deliberately, "Of course I put my teeth in. After all, I was going out," and she closed her mouth firmly, her nostrils flaring wide.

I was so consumed by the desire to get a better look at her white, even teeth that I forgot to blink. Then I noticed a strange hissing sound. Miss Sasaki was holding both hands to her eyes and seemed to be groaning in agony. Beside her, my mother was staring intently at the ground, her shoulders shaking. At first I thought they were crying, but it appeared that in fact they were laughing. Not understanding what was so funny, I looked over at Mr. Nishioka. His little eyes darted about and his eyebrows were twitching violently. The landlady entered her house and closed the door with a firm click.

After supper, the adults took me to her house and made me apologize, despite the fact that I didn't have a clue as to why she was so upset. By this time, I knew that she had just been wearing false teeth. (Oh, is that all? I thought, disappointed) and I was very relieved to know that she was all right. Personally, I thought that she looked better without her teeth, and I felt vexed, as though I had lost something. After that, I was so tired that for once I slept through the night without dreaming.

# Chapter 6

Father,

How are you? Yesterday I went to the eye doctor's to look for the landlady. On the way home, I thought of you. I remembered the time I went to the zoo with Yuta and his mother, and you came to the train station to meet me. You held my hand and smoked a cigarette and told me a story about a rabbit who lives on the moon. Once there were some hungry people and the animals brought them food. But the rabbit was too weak to carry anything and so instead he jumped into the flames and let the people eat him. You told me that the dead rabbit rose to the moon. After you finished the story, I thought about it as I lay in bed. And I cried a little. I don't like sad stories very much. Last night I thought that maybe you are on the moon with the rabbit and I cried a lot more. I

*think it must be lonely on the moon with just you*
*and the rabbit.*

*When the landlady's drawer is full, she will die.*
*So I've decided not to write to you every day. In-*
*stead, when I do write, I will write very small. I'll*
*make my pencil very sharp and write lots.*

*Goodbye for now.*

I still wrote to my father, and ironically, despite the fact that I had been thrown into a panic believing the landlady to be dead on the day she went to the wake, I wrote with even more zeal than before. The thought that she might die at any moment changed my letter writing, which had originally begun as play and quickly become a familiar habit, into something else, something much more urgent. In my letters I had finally begun to speak directly to my father.

Perhaps I had recovered enough so that it no longer caused me pain to think of him. But it was more that I was trying to understand some secret I could not unravel on my own. Even now that I have grown up, whenever I sense that something is out of place I cannot let the issue rest, no matter how insignificant it may be, until I have followed the trail back to the very beginning, rather like when one's shirt buttons are done up in the wrong order, even though at times it means opening old wounds. This character trait may be what caused my mother and me to grow so far apart after she remarried and tried to create a new existence for herself. But whatever the reason, one day I wrote:

*Father,*

*How are you? My toenails are just like your toenails. I know that because you once told me so. I looked at your toenails then and thought they really do look the same. Today Mother cut my toenails after my bath. As I was looking at them, I had a strange feeling. I have toenails but you don't. You don't have toenails but my toenails are like yours. Before, there was you and Mother and I, so why is it that now only you have gone and Mother and I are still here? But when I think about this a lot, my mind goes around in circles.*

*While Mother cut my nails, she wrinkled her brow and looked very serious. I thought, What did my father's face look like when he cut my nails? But I could not remember. It must have been because you were looking down the whole time. I liked it better when you cut my nails. Why? Because you cut them very slowly, which meant that it didn't tickle.*

*Goodbye for now.*

The month of December was already half over and the winter vacation was here. On the last day of the term I came running home from school in the clear winter sunshine. As I ran up the stairs, I saw a boy I had never seen before standing in front of Mr. Nishioka's washing machine. He looked like a tall, slender white mushroom with spectacles. He seemed older than I and was shoving a huge pile of laundry into the machine.

The first thing that came to my mind was the washing machine incident. Although I could hardly believe that the same thing might happen again, I hesitated before opening our door and instead stood there staring.

"Hello," he said, in a slightly hoarse but cheerful voice. Without answering, I went inside. I picked up the lunch of rice balls my mother had prepared for me and peeked through a crack in the door. He was loading the machine as if he was quite accustomed to it. I went outside and locked the door, making sure to avoid his eyes, and then dashed down the stairs.

"Mrs. Yanagi, there's a strange boy upstairs."

With her reading glasses on, the landlady had no difficulty deciphering even the finest newsprint, and one of her daily pleasures was to read the newspaper from beginning to end. That day she was sitting at the *kotatsu* with the newspaper spread out in front of her. When I spoke to her she said, "Strange boy?" She peered up at me over her glasses, which had slipped down her nose, and the wrinkles in her brow bunched together.

"He wears glasses. And he was doing his laundry in Mr. Nishioka's washing machine."

"That's Mr. Nishioka's boy," she said.

"Mr. Nishioka has children?"

"Yes, he does."

"But—"

"He lives with his mother." She leaned over the *kotatsu* and gathered up the newspaper, tapping it sharply against the tabletop. As she didn't seem to be encouraging any more questions, I fell silent.

I had finished lunch and was by the laundry rack feeding the cats some leftover fish from last night's supper when I heard light footsteps coming down the apartment stairs. Walking through the garden and around to the landlady's front door, I found that, just as I had suspected, it was the boy.

"Is Mrs. Yanagi here?" When I nodded, he followed me into the garden. Through the sliding glass door, he handed the landlady a box stamped with the words "Loquat Jelly" and said in a grownup tone of voice, "Please accept this humble gift."

"Why, thank you," the landlady said solemnly, and she bowed slowly and deliberately. "Oh, by the way, this is Chiaki, your next-door neighbor. She's in first grade."

Then she turned to me and told me briefly that his name was Osamu and that he was in fourth grade. He seemed small for a fourth grader. "He's here for the holidays, Chiaki, so be sure to ask him to play with you."

Instead of saying yes, I looked at Osamu and saw that he was pursing his lips like someone who is trying to suppress a laugh, hiding his overly large front teeth. He said he was going to buy ingredients to make curry, and I decided to go with him. We walked down the road beside the creek kicking a stone back and forth between us. In his thinness and the way he walked with his back slightly stooped and head bobbing, he resembled Mr. Nishioka.

"I'm very good at making curry."

"Really? You can make curry by yourself?" I was impressed, although I supposed that all fourth graders must be able to. "Did your mother teach you?"

"Yeah, but I usually get recipes from books or TV. My mom works as a tutor, so she's always busy."

"My mom works at a wedding hall. She gets to see brides every day. Lots of them."

"Hmm."

"Do you like brides?"

He thought for a minute and then said, "Not really."

"Why?"

"They're sort of creepy. You know, with all that stuff they wear."

Osamu did the shopping with a practiced air at a super-market in the arcade, and then we walked home together along the creek. I still remember how I prattled on until we reached the apartment, completely forgetting my usual shyness with strangers, telling him all about the landlady and about how Miss Sasaki threw food to the cats. Osamu giggled sometimes as he listened, or, when I was at a loss for words, asked me a helpful question. For a fourth grader, he was an excellent listener.

"When the curry's ready, would you like to eat with us?" he asked when we reached the corridor outside our apartments. I wanted to say, Yes! but didn't. I thought it wouldn't be fair to my mother without getting her permission first.

"Well, how about going to church?"

"Church?"

"To Christmas mass." It was not that I didn't know it was Christmas Eve. But because I had always believed that Santa Claus was really my father, I just didn't expect that we would ever be able to celebrate Christmas again. That evening, however, my mother brought home a cake covered in whipped cream and strawberries. I put two slices on a plate and knocked on Mr. Nishioka's door. Inside, he and Osamu were sitting across from each other at a small folding table and eating curry.

Mr. Nishioka took the cake and thanked me. "Chiaki,

what did your mother say?" he asked. "Can you come to church with us?"

"My mother wants to come, too. Is that okay?"

"Of course it's okay. Let's go together."

Osamu looked at me and grinned with the curry spoon still gripped in his hand. I bet that curry is good, I thought.

"In that case, you'd better have a rest before you go, Chiaki. It will be very late," Mr. Nishioka said. But I was so excited at the idea of going out in the middle of the night that, although I lay down, it was impossible to sleep.

"Mom, Mr. Nishioka and Osamu were eating curry."

"They were?"

"It was like camping."

"Camping?"

"They were eating quietly, just the two of them."

"Chiaki."

"Mm."

"It's not polite to stare at people when they're eating."

"Yes, I know. It really was like camping."

"Yes, yes."

What I wanted to say was that there was something special about the way the two of them were eating together, but I could not think of any better way of describing it. Camping for me was something only glimpsed occasionally on television. The gentle glow of firelight in the darkness, silent people eating simple warm food, the sounds of night birds, a sky filled with stars . . . I suddenly realized that for once Mr. Nishioka wasn't playing his comedy tapes.

We left Poplar House late. The night sky was clear and the stars were glimmering way up high like living creatures. My mother dressed me in a warm sweater, then wrapped me up in a coat and wool scarf, and even made me wear a wool hat. I must have looked like a stuffed animal about to burst at the seams.

"Are you a Christian, Mr. Nishioka?" my mother asked.

"No, not me," he said hastily and then added, "but my boy has been baptized because his mother is a Christian." And he rested the flat of his palm on Osamu's head. "She kept pushing me to become one, before we got married. But I'm glad that I didn't."

"Why?"

He seemed surprised that my mother should ask such an innocent question. "Well, you know . . . D-don't you see? Catholics can't get d-d-divorced."

"Oh!"

"She kept telling me to become a believer, and then she was the one who walked out," he said as if to himself, and laughed soundlessly. "But it all happened long ago," he remarked, his voice back at its normal rapid pace.

The church was located down the road along the creek

and then up a fairly steep hill near the fire station on the opposite side from the shopping arcade. Looking back from the top of the hill, I could clearly see the cluster of neon lights around the station reflected in the darkness of the big river. A train, crammed with men in suits illuminated in minute and crowded detail, crossed the bridge over the river. My mother stood staring vacantly at the train, and I pulled at her hand.

We were in a much classier residential area than where we lived, and the houses with their majestic gates were dark and silent. The churchyard, which was overshadowed by the branches of a single oak, appeared to be completely dark, but when we opened the heavy wooden doors, light and music flooded out and both my mother and I caught our breath.

The inside of the church was warm, and everyone was standing up, singing. Osamu put the tip of his finger in what looked like a washbasin carved from white stone and made the sign of the cross. Then he looked at me as if to say I should try it, too. The water was cold to the touch. Osamu took my hand and made the sign of the cross for me.

I heard songs, organ music, and pleasant verses praising our Father, God. The ceiling was very high, just like a cake box packed full of resonant sound. For a while I mimicked what everyone else did—standing, kneeling, sitting—

as if I had lost my own volition, but before I realized it my eyes were fastened on the cross at the front of the church.

"Who's that?" I whispered to Osamu.

"Jesus Christ." His breath smelled like toothpaste.

"Why is he naked?"

Osamu just shrugged.

"Is he dead?"

"Yes, well . . ."

"Why?"

"He died to save us."

The organ hummed to life once again and people began to sing. Osamu wore a very solemn face, and his voice when he sang was just like when he talked, high and slightly hoarse. Mr. Nishioka stared at the black leather-bound hymnal and moved his mouth a little. When I looked at my mother, her eyes were moist, like those of someone who was drunk.

I felt sympathy for this Jesus Christ with his emaciated body and his face so full of suffering. It can't be much fun to be exposed naked in front of all these people, I thought. Then I remembered the rabbit that my father had told me about. The rabbit had died for a god that had appeared before him as a hungry man, and Osamu had said that this Christ died for us. When someone dies, is it always to help someone else? I wondered. For what purpose did my father die? For someone who was hungry? For mankind? For Mother? Or, perhaps, for me?

When the talk about God began, I was suddenly over-come with drowsiness. When my mother shook me awake, there was almost nobody left inside the church. The woman who had played the organ was gathering to-gether her music. The glittering cake-box church now looked like just any old meeting hall.

The air outside was so cold it stung my eyes. I turned once more at the open doors and looked back at Jesus Christ on the cross.

"Are you going to leave me here like this?" he asked.

"I'll come again," I whispered, and went outside.

❧

Since Mr. Nishioka often started work in the evenings, Osamu went shopping in the afternoon and made supper early. I followed Osamu around every day, sometimes car-rying a little of the shopping, sometimes helping him wash vegetables. Osamu standing in the kitchen wearing an apron, a ladle gripped in his right hand as he reached for a bottle of soy sauce with his left, looked exactly like a middle-aged housewife. Just as blankets that have been slept in always remind me of alligators. No matter how hard I rubbed my eyes to see if I was just imagining things, I could not dispel this image. And being in the kitchen with this "housewife" was fun and reassuring.

I think this had something to do with the fact that I never felt at ease when watching my mother in the kitchen. Although I know it is unjust to my mother, who struggled to make my meals every day, I was choking with the constant anxiety that, overworked and overtired, she would one day disappear and leave me as my father had. I learned how to use the washing machine and fold the laundry, and I volunteered to buy the milk every day, but although I did the best a first grader could be expected to do, no matter how I tried, every time I saw my mother working at the sink, I dreaded being left behind. The most apt description of my mother during that period was someone imprisoned within her own fear.

Mind you, Osamu was not working in the kitchen simply for the joy of it, either. One day as we walked home from shopping, I said to him, "You should stay here forever."

"Uh-huh, maybe I will."

Totally unprepared for such a felicitous response, I was thrown into ecstasy. "Oh yes, do. Do!"

"After all, I am a better cook than my dad."

"Uh-huh, uh-huh."

"And when the baby's born, my mother will be very busy."

"She's going to have a baby?"

"Yes. The due date is January third."

"Ohh."

"My mother's not that strong, so she's already been hospitalized."

So that's why he's here, I nodded to myself. "Why don't you go to visit her at New Year's?" I suggested.

"It's too far."

"But she'll be lonely by herself."

"My father will be there."

"What?"

"My new father. Not this one."

I said, "Oh!" like a dimwit, and then walked along in silence as I tried to sort things out in my head. "Is your new father mean to you?"

"No," he answered simply, shaking his head. I was greatly relieved, as if it were me personally, for I had been imagining the wicked stepmothers found in fairy tales. Yet something still bothered me.

"You know, I really like that apartment," Osamu announced abruptly, his long narrow eyes widening behind his glasses. "Mrs. Yanagi reminds me of my grandmother. When I was little, I stayed with my grandmother once. I haven't seen her in a long time, though."

"Yeah?" I found it incredible that his grandmother could possibly have such a mean-looking face.

"Maybe it's because she calls me 'Mr. Osamu.' My grandma used to say, 'Mr. Osamu, the peaches are nice and cold.' She was really nice." He stared straight ahead at a spot about three yards in front of his toes and snapped his index finger against his large front teeth.

"Osamu, do you know anybody who has died?"

"No. Why?"

"Oh, nothing."

I had had this compelling urge to tell Osamu about the letters and the landlady's drawer. But if no one he knew had died, then it was better to keep it a secret between me and Mrs. Yanagi. I felt a strange mixture of disappointment and relief, and kicked one foot high up into the air. My shoes were getting too small.

❧

*Father,*

*How are you? Today Osamu said, "I'll pick the snake gourds for you." He tried to climb the poplar tree. But there are no branches low down and he was standing there wondering what to do when the landlady asked him, "What are you doing?" Osamu said, "I want to get the snake gourds but I can't climb the tree," and so she went to the shed and got him the gardening shears. They are clippers with really long handles. "My Professor bought these from a gardening shop when he was alive," she told us. Osamu turned the pickling jar upside down and stood on top of it. Then he said, "Oof!" and lifted the shears. They just barely reached the bottom gourd. Osamu's arms were shaking like crazy. He finally cut the gourd and I caught it as it fell. "Nice catch!"*

Osamu said in a loud voice. I felt really happy. But after that, the shears were so heavy Osamu fell over.

The snake gourd was very shiny. I thought that it would be soft like a tomato but it wasn't. When I asked if you can eat them, the landlady said, "Why don't you try it?" But when I started to take a bite, Osamu said, "Chiaki, you'd better not," and I stopped. The landlady said, "Was she really going to eat it?" and that made me mad.

I said we should take the snake gourd to the church and give it to the man on the cross because it was so pretty. Osamu said that it was a good idea. It was a little scary going into the church when nobody was there. Osamu said, "When someone dies, they go to God's country. You'll go there, too, Chiaki. Me, too." God is a shepherd and people are his sheep. I tried to imagine you as a sheep, Father. But I can't believe it. I don't like to think of you all by yourself up on the moon with just a rabbit, but I don't want you to be a sheep either. If you become a sheep, I don't think I will be able to tell you apart from all the other ones.

Jesus was naked and all by himself. He looked bored. I put the snake gourd under the cross. Then I ran outside, where it occurred to me that Jesus is just *a little bit like you. He looks more like you than your picture on our altar at home. But I think that is kind of strange.*

*Osamu said that next time we should bring flowers. I'd like to go again. But if it were me, I'd prefer snake gourds to flowers. I think if someone asked you that, you would also say you like snake gourds better.*

*Goodbye for now.*

FOR THE NEXT FEW DAYS, while the town around us was bustling with preparations for the New Year—music spewing out into the streets, and people and bicycles racing about distractedly—the landlady, Osamu, and I spent our time as if the commotion around us didn't exist.

Osamu and I were absorbed in taking offerings to the church—a pretty colored leaf, pinecones, a picture of an airplane that Osamu drew, a button that looked like a piece of candy from a suit my mother used to wear—and laying them at the foot of the cross. At times, the wooden Christ looked to me as if he had simply had a little mishap, like he'd dropped his wallet or stepped in some dog doo, rather than as if he were suffering. Drawn to the mysterious fact that his expression seemed different every time I saw him, I climbed the long road up the hill to the church two and even three times a day, inviting Osamu to accompany me. Every time I said, "Let's go," Osamu always responded, "Okay, let's," which made me very happy. Perhaps Osamu's willingness helped make the game so much fun for me.

The landlady did not seem to be in any hurry to prepare for New Year's. If you'd asked me, I'd have had to say that she seemed to be spending each and every day collecting cat poop. The cats usually did their business in a corner of the yard and covered it up neatly when they were finished, but apparently there was one who did not, and sometimes there was cat poop scattered about right in the middle of the yard. The landlady, with her passion for being tidy, could not stand to leave it lying around. Wearing work gloves and carrying a paper bag and a trowel, she wandered about the yard, her eyes gleaming and her nostrils flaring. She called Osamu and me over when we were about to go out and said, "Here," shoving the paper bag under our noses. When we screwed up our faces at the awful odor, she seemed satisfied, exclaiming, "Aha, just as I thought." Osamu and I looked at each other, puzzled, and the land-lady put her nose into the bag so that only her white hair was showing and nodded, muttering, "It smells. My nose still works." I guessed that she was losing her sense of smell.

Because we were in mourning that year, my mother and I did not write any New Year's cards, but we did spend

New Year's Eve and New Year's Day at the home of my mother's eldest brother, Hiroyuki. My uncle lived with my Aunt Toshiko and my two cousins, and also with my grandmother, who had moved in with them recently. My mother almost never went to this brother's house. It was not that they did not like each other. It was just that they did not have much in common. But Uncle Hiroyuki insisted that we should come and visit my grandmother at least for New Year's Day, and as the three-hour journey, which required changing trains several times, was too long for a day trip, we ended up staying the night. As my uncle pointed out, it was ages since we had seen my grandmother. She had not even been able to come to my father's funeral because she was hospitalized with a liver ailment.

My mother and her brother sipped beer and watched the New Year's Eve special on TV, conversing listlessly. My two teenage cousins sang and danced in front of the television, mimicking the performers on the variety show. And I sat drowsily at the *kotatsu*, wondering what Osamu was doing.

My aunt treated my grandmother like a baby. She used an almost sickly-sweet tone of voice when speaking to her. "Here you are, Grandma. There's a good girl. Eat some melon, now." Although my grandmother was still perfectly capable of doing it herself, Aunt Toshiko cut the melon up into bite-size pieces for her. My grandmother was very petite and she did look rather cute as she sat there with a vacant smile, wearing a fluffy mohair sweater that matched her fair skin. It seemed that the more my aunt used her babying voice, the more like a baby my grandmother became. As I watched her, for some reason I recalled our landlady, looking rather slovenly as she stood in the kitchen with only her apron crisp and neat, repeatedly reheating and sipping her foul-tasting brew of miso soup.

"Mom," I said after we had crawled onto our futons, "what time are we going home tomorrow?" I was a restless sleeper anyway, but those futon covers were positively stiff with starch.

My mother turned over and looked at me. "You want to go home?"

"No, it's not that."

"It's not that, but you want to go home."

"Yeah."

"Me, too."

"Really?"

My mother nodded. It seemed like a long time since I had talked with her like this, and I felt glad.

"Grandma sure has grown old," she said, as if to herself. "Everyone is going to leave me," she whispered, and then, turning her back to me, she began to weep quietly.

I slid out of my futon and crawled into her bed, snuggling my back up against hers. After I started kindergarten, my mother rarely let me sleep with her, but that night was different. The warmth of her body gradually seeped into mine and suddenly, in the depths of my tightly closed eyes, I saw my father's face vividly. His eyes were shut and he looked pensive. Yes, I remembered. My father often closed his eyes like that while he smoked or sometimes while he listened to music. I wanted to know what it was he was thinking about. But whenever I approached him, his eyes would pop open and he would pick me up. So, although that in itself made me happy, I was never able to enter the thoughts he pondered while alone.

"I'm sorry." Rubbing the tears from her eyes like a child, my mother turned toward me. "Did I shock you?"

I shook my head. "No. Mom?"

"Yes."

"I've been writing letters. To Father."

There was a moment's silence and then my mother said, "I see. You're writing letters to your father."

"They'll be taken to him. Really." If she had asked me by whom, I felt I would have told her the whole story, but she said nothing and stared at the tips of my fingers, which lay in her hand.

Then she asked, "What do you write?"

"Umm."

"Your secrets?"

"I write some secrets. And also about Osamu and things like that."

My mother laughed softly.

"Mom, Dad never got angry, did he?"

"No," she said, but her voice was somehow distracted.

"When I write to him, it feels sort of strange."

"Why strange?"

"I think, My father died. He really died. But it doesn't feel frightening anymore."

"Were you afraid before?"

"Yeah."

We were silent for a while. "Would you like to write to him, Mom?"

"Maybe sometime."

"When you do, tell me. I'll take your letter to be delivered." I closed my eyes quickly, hoping to fall asleep before she told me to get back into my own bed. But it seemed she had no intention of doing so. She pressed her nose against my short, recently cropped hair and stayed still for a long time. And as I lay there feigning sleep, I fell into a deep slumber.

On New Year's Day, my mother and I ended up taking my grandmother for a walk. Going for a walk after breakfast was part of her daily routine, and regardless of whether or not it was New Year's, she wasn't about to change this habit. My aunt, however, was suffering from the effects of drinking a little sake in the morning to celebrate the

New Year. My uncle kept unsuccessfully nagging her to "hurry up and take her for a walk, will you?" as if my grandmother were some pet his wife was looking after. My two cousins had both gone out with friends to visit a shrine.

We set off for a nearby park, matching our stride to my grandmother's slower pace. The whole town was wrapped in a peaceful quiet appropriate to New Year's Day, and the air was tight and crisp like the clear winter sky. My grandmother said nothing. When my mother asked her, "Are you cold?" or "Is this the way you usually go?" she just shook her head or nodded. I doubted that she even knew who we were. She had not spoken our names once since our arrival the day before.

We sat down on a sunny bench in the park. A cat was digging a hole in the sandbox in front of us to do his business.

"Look, Mother. There's a cat. A cat," my mother said, pointing for my grandmother. Taking her cue from my aunt, she had started speaking to my grandmother as if she were a child, so what my grandmother said next came as quite a shock to both of us.

"Please stop that." She snorted through her nose in disgust.

"Stop what?" my mother asked, blinking in surprise.

"Listening to you use that wheedling tone is going to put me in an early grave."

Our mouths dropped open. Where was that sweet little old lady who was here a minute ago?

"How old are you now?" As my mother just stared at her with her mouth open, Grandma repeated the question, "I said, how old are you?"

"Thirty-seven."

She nodded at my mother's reply. After groping about in a plastic bag that rested on her lap, she brought out a fat envelope and handed it to my mother.

"What's this?" my mother asked, and then, as she peered inside, she exclaimed, "Why, it's money!"

"I figured that if I waited until I died, you wouldn't get much."

"But what about Hiroyuki and his family?"

"That's for me to worry about, not you." My grandmother's voice was rapidly growing firmer and clearer. "You need money, don't you?"

"Yes, of course, but . . . Thank you. Thank you very much. It will really help." In addition to the money, the envelope also held a round gold ring.

"I bought that before you were born. It must be more than forty years old now."

My mother tried it on. It fit perfectly on her middle finger. "You were already forty-two when I was born, right? Amazing."

My mother sat gazing at the ring on her hand. My grandmother did not respond to her question but instead looked at her steadily, almost as if she were inspecting her. "When you reach your age, you feel like you are old already, don't you?"

My mother laughed briefly, then responded with a vague, "Yeah, I guess so."

"Well, perhaps times are different now, but that's what I felt like. I felt depressed. Your father was doing well at the company and strutted about confidently. You weren't born yet, but he had a woman."

"A woman? My father?"

"Yes."

"That's impossible. He always turned the TV off whenever there was a romance on."

"Even so, he had a mistress. So what with that, I felt like my life was over. To cheer myself up, for the first time ever I bought something for myself without telling him. It felt wonderful. That's what I bought, that ring."

My mother was staring at it. I did not understand exactly what they were talking about, but my attention became riveted to my grandmother's face. Her eyes, her mouth, even her nostrils seemed twice as large as when she was in the house.

"After that, things gradually got better, and then you were born. So it's a lucky ring, you see." I had been listening intently to this adult conversation, and now she turned to me and winked. "Isn't it pretty? When you grow up, your mother will give it to you."

My mother held out her hand toward me. I could see my face, stretched out sideways, reflected in the smooth gold surface. "I know things must be difficult for you now," my grandmother said to my mother. She stopped to clear her throat. "But your life ahead of you is what matters. Don't waste it. I don't want you to look back later and realize you were still young and could have done something more."

My mother nodded repeatedly as if to say, I know. "I'll be all right," she said.

"Really? When I saw you wearing that old suit yesterday, I was shocked."

The fact that my mother's checkered suit had met with disapproval came as a complete surprise to me. It was my favorite. My mother laughed aloud. "I actually wore that on purpose. After all, I am in mourning. You know Hiroyuki's very particular."

"Oh, that boy. He's so rigid. A real stickler for propriety." She made a wry face. "I have no choice but to play the aged grandma. If I didn't, things just wouldn't work out." She shook her head sharply when my mother began to protest. "Everyone knows what I'm really like, just an old chatterbox. My hairdresser, Dr. Naganuma, Mr. Tashiro the mailman, Mrs. Yoshigiwa from the seniors' association, Mrs. Tamiya. But they're all very understanding. They never let on in front of Toshiko that I'm just pretending. They're all very good people."

It was my grandmother who first stood up and said, "Well, shall we go, then?" Even now I can distinctly recall the change that came over her face the instant we passed through the gate of my uncle's house, as if she had put on a mask; her eyes sank back into their sockets and her mouth became pursed. We were served tea immediately upon our return, and my grandmother pecked like a bird at a firm sweet jelly my aunt had chopped into ridiculously small pieces for her.

*Father,*

*How are you? Today I went with Osamu and his father to the river and we flew kites. Osamu's father ran a lot and our kites flew very high. The river wind was very cold. But Osamu and I were hot because we ran so much.*

*Mr. Nishioka cut his hair short. You can see the bald spot on his head clearly now. But he looks much younger than before.*

*Osamu told his father he wants to stay here. And his father said okay. But Osamu can't come right away. He has to go home first but will move back during spring vacation. I was so happy I grabbed Osamu's hands, and we whirled round and round and ran along the river beach.*

When we finished flying kites, we went to the church. I found a pretty brooch at the park I went to with Grandma when we stayed at Uncle Hiroyuki's. I gave it to Jesus. The pin is broken but it has a red jewel in it that shines and it is really pretty. I thought Jesus would look happy if I did that. But he looked like he was thinking about something else. I asked him, "What are you thinking about?" but he didn't answer. On the way home I said to Osamu, "I hate Jesus," and he got mad and said, "How can you say that?" I said, "Because he's dead." Osamu said, "He is not dead." Then I hit him. Osamu didn't hit me but he wouldn't talk to me.

At nighttime, I went and said sorry to Osamu. Osamu said, "I'm not angry," and I was glad.

Then I played rock-paper-scissors with Osamu on the stairs outside. I love being there at night because the light for the stairway is on and everywhere else is dark. While we played, Miss Sasaki came home carrying a big suitcase. She had been to Hawaii. She gave Osamu and me chocolates as a present. We ate them together, one at a time. They were really good.

Goodbye for now.

The day before school started, Osamu took his suitcase and went home. I wanted to go with Mr. Nishioka and see him off, but I had to say goodbye at the gate of the apartment house because Mr. Nishioka was going directly to work afterward. All I could think about was that Osamu would be back in the spring. He would live with Mr. Nishioka and play with me every day.

On the day the news announced the arrival of the worst cold spell of the year, I came home to find a letter from Osamu in our mailbox.

*January 23*

*Dear Chiaki,*

*How are you? I am well, but this letter is not going to be a very nice one. At first I thought I had better not write, but I will anyway because I want to tell you.*

*My mother finally got out of the hospital. But the baby is dead. It was born all right, but its lungs didn't work properly and it died soon after.*

*My mother cries every day. My father (I mean the one here) is also very disappointed. But he has to work, so he cannot stay with my mother much.*

*I make rice porridge for her every day. She only eats a little. When I feed her, she says thank you, and she eats just a bit, crying all the time. Lately she talks about when she was a little girl. She talks for an hour, sometimes two, and then she falls asleep, as if she is very tired.*

*Chiaki, I promised that I would move there in the spring but I cannot keep my promise. I cannot leave my mother for a while. I think she would be too sad if after she lost the baby, I left, too. I'm sorry. My father (the one at Poplar House) says, "You should be with your mother." He says, "I am used to being alone. I'll be fine." But I know that he gets lonely, and I am a little worried. Please take care of him for me, Chiaki.*

*I will write again. I would like to go with you to the church again. I am really sorry that I can't keep my promise.*

Osamu Endo


I ran straight to the landlady's house and thrust the letter at her as she was ironing. "Osamu's mother told him she didn't need him anymore because she was having a new baby. But just because the baby's dead, she changes her mind. That's not fair! Poor Osamu!"

I buried my face in the landlady's apron, which smelled of detergent and green tea, and drenched it with my tears, runny nose, and spittle. I don't know how long I stayed like that. When I finally lifted my face from her lap, she fed me sweet-chestnut-and-bean jelly. As I swallowed the food, my throat all gummed up with tears and snot, I felt suddenly ravenous.

The landlady sliced a piece of jelly with a fruit knife and ate it, cut another piece and fed it to me. Although her consumption of sweets usually left me dumbfounded, this time I was a match for her, even though I knew that this particular jelly was one she had specially ordered from an acquaintance. Before you could blink an eye, we had polished off one whole stick and then another, during which time we spoke not a word.

When I had become sufficiently intoxicated by sugar, the landlady glanced at my face and said, "All right." I hadn't a clue as to just what was "all right," but I found myself fuming, "Mrs. Yanagi, I'm going to write Osamu a letter. I'm going to say, 'Definitely let's play together again.'"

"That's a good idea. There aren't many boys as good as Osamu, you know."

As it turned out, Osamu never came back to Poplar House while I was there, and our correspondence, which was after all between children, did not last long. But I still remember, even now, some of the earnest phrases he wrote. Once he sent me a photograph. It was from a school excursion, and it showed him making a V sign with his fingers and managing somehow to smile as he stood, very tense, beside a chained baby bear. I liked that photo because it seemed so true to Osamu's character.

## Chapter 8

*I*S THERE A DOCTOR ON BOARD?"

Although I am sleeping, the low but penetrating voice reaches my ears. It takes me a moment to realize that it is the flight attendant speaking. I glance at my watch and see that forty minutes have passed since takeoff. I must have fallen sound asleep. After my mother's phone call last night when I had learned that Mrs. Yanagi was dead, a flood of memories had kept me awake.

"Excuse me, I'm a nurse." I regret the words as soon as I have spoken them. True, I was a nurse but I quit my job. And what if the situation exceeds my capability?

"Could you come this way, please? One of the passengers is suffering from severe stomach pain."

As she speaks, she deftly refastens my tray table, which I had left open, into the back of the seat in front of me as if she has not noticed my hesitation. We pass through the curtain that partitions off the front part of the plane. The seats here are more spacious, and on one, which has been put in the reclining position, lies a young girl of about fifteen. As soon as I see her thin form, wrapped in blankets and obviously rigid with pain, my hesitancy vanishes.

The flight attendant informs me that the girl is traveling alone. When the girl learns that I am a nurse, her expression relaxes slightly.

"Can you tell me what happened?" I ask.

"I suddenly had this terrible pain in my stomach . . . and then I threw up."

"Where does it hurt?" I ask, rolling down the blanket. She places her hand on top of her abdomen and says, "Here." Undoing the belt of her jeans, I explore the area, placing the palm of my hand against her skin, which is slightly damp with sweat.

"Here?"

"Mmm."

Then I move my hand to the right and down from where she has indicated and press firmly.

"Ow!"

"What was your vomit like?"

"I threw up in the toilet."

"Was there blood mixed in with it?"

"I don't think so. It was white."

I draw a deep breath of relief. I ask for her home phone number, and fortunately it seems to be an area code near our destination.

The flight attendant says diffidently that they have stomach medicine and painkillers, but I shake my head. "It may be appendicitis. Can you arrange for an ambulance to meet us at the airport?" Her eyes, beautifully made up, catch mine and hold, as if to say, I trust you. And you can trust me.

"Yes, we can. I'll contact them right away. Is there anything else?"

"This is her home phone number. Oh, also, if you have a thermometer and more blankets, could you bring them, please."

"Sure."

The girl, groaning with pain, looks up at me uneasily.

"You're going to be fine. We'll be landing in about thirty minutes." I kneel down in the aisle and take her hand.

"You think it's my appendix?"

"Yes, but we won't know for sure until they check you out at a hospital."

"If it's just my appendix, that's okay. My mother had hers out. I don't want to have a scar, though."

"They may not even need to operate, you know. The first thing you have to do is see a doctor." She nods. I stay there holding her hand and talking to her to distract her a little. She tells me, between gasps of pain, that she went to visit her father, who is living on his own because of a business transfer. I wonder what could have taken her to her father's when school wasn't out. Even as I comfort her, I cannot help thinking such things.

The first time I knew that I wanted to be a nurse was when I was about her age. I had gone to the hospital to visit my grandmother, who by that time was dying, and had been completely smitten with one of the nurses.

I can still clearly remember her slender figure dressed in a white uniform. I had never been able to imagine myself as an adult, and it was she who finally gave me something resembling a vision of my future. Her calm and dedicated air, her precise movements, the pleasant sense of vitality that underlay her modest speech—all these things, I thought feverishly at fifteen, can only belong to someone who firmly believes in herself. This encounter was particularly meaningful because, despite the fact that I was always at the top of my class regardless of how little I studied, and despite my experiments with wearing makeup and riding on the back of the motorcycle of some guy in his senior year, I was certain that I could never find that kind of confidence.

Looking back now, I think that nursing was in fact her calling. She could turn my bedridden grandmother, which was heavy labor, more briskly and considerately than any-

one else. When she came into the room, my grandmother's face relaxed as if with heartfelt relief. And then
my grandmother would begin talking about her youth,
telling stories that I, her own granddaughter, had not heard
even once before, about how she had been a typist, a very
stylish job for a young woman in her day, and so forth.

But my encounter with that nurse was not the only reason I decided that that's what I wanted to be. Around the
same time, I had already begun thinking about leaving
home as soon as possible. I felt I would suffocate if I did
not extricate myself quickly from my mixed-up feelings
for my mother. Whenever I brought up the subject of my
dead father, she would recount innocuous memories, yet
somewhere I could still sense that her heart was closed, and
this I resented. But just when I thought I couldn't stand it
any longer, I would feel in myself such a willingness to die
for her sake that it reduced me to tears. My poor, sweet
mother who had suffered so, and who now left everything
up to my stepfather, never even attempting to make any
decisions for herself. Then I would get irritated by this
woman who had allowed herself to grow plump after re-
marrying, as though she no longer had anything to worry
about. And the same voice kept swirling around in my
mind: Is she really happy? Or is she just pretending to be
happy?

I was constantly brooding about leaving home, despite
the fact that until I visited my grandmother in the hospital

I hadn't the least clue as to what kind of adult I wanted to be, and so for me nursing seemed the perfect profession. Perhaps I am now being punished. Is it because the motives in my heart at fifteen years of age were impure that I ended up quitting my job at the hospital and feeling as if there is nowhere left to go?

I hear the announcement to prepare for landing, and the girl's sweaty hand squeezes my own tightly.

"We'll be landing in a minute," I reassure her. I place my hand on the thin flesh of her stomach. The pain seems to transmit itself directly to me, and for an instant I feel stunned. She is very tough, much more so than I had thought.

"Please keep your hand there," she says faintly, her eyes still closed.

That's just it. Although I worked twice as enthusiastically as anyone else, I was never a particularly good nurse. Sometimes, even as I coaxed and reassured grown men who wept with fear before a simple operation like having their appendix out, I was all the while looking upon them with contempt. So why do I feel this girl's pain so vividly? Why now, when I have vowed never to return to nursing?

Even after the plane lands and the girl is placed in the ambulance and taken away, the hot pain lingers in my hand. In the middle of the huge lobby of the brand-new airport, I stand for a while pretending to gaze at the flight information board, clenching my hand in my pocket.

## Chapter 9

T WAS AT SETSUBUN, a festival marking the bitter end of winter and the coming of spring, not long after I had received Osamu's letter, that Mr. Nishioka got into trouble.

He met with a friend and the two of them went out drinking. This friend, who was a chef by trade, originally met Mr. Nishioka while working temporarily as a taxi driver and had recently started working as a chef again. His old habit of playing truant from work, however, had manifested itself and he was fired. He had complained to Mr. Nishioka and even wept in front of him, claiming that this time he had meant to do his best but had been fired, and wasn't the world a cold, cruel place.

Mr. Nishioka was a kind man at heart. Fueled by the liquor he had drunk, he declared, "I'll talk to them for you," and went off to visit the restaurant from which his friend had been fired. At first he assumed a humble attitude and was even willing to kneel down on the floor and plead. The woman who ran the establishment not only snubbed him coldly but had the gall to make some caustic remark about him, and Mr. Nishioka flew into a rage. Normally he would never have allowed something like that to upset him, and I suspect that his mind was in turmoil because of Osamu.

It wasn't until the next day that the police contacted the landlady. Mr. Nishioka had called the taxi company where he worked first, but the company was completely indifferent to his plight. The landlady asked Miss Sasaki to accompany her to the station, pulled out a kimono that smelled of camphor, changed, deliberated over whether to wear her false teeth or not, and finally left without them. "You take care of the house while I'm gone," she said to me.

They soon returned with Mr. Nishioka. His face was deathly pale and he staggered up the steps like a ghost. "Terrible hangover," Miss Sasaki remarked, frowning, as she watched him go.

I learned the details by eavesdropping on the conversation between the landlady and Miss Sasaki. Whether because she had an unexpected streak of compassion or was inspired instead by curiosity, Miss Sasaki took on the task of phoning people for the landlady. Although you would never know it, the landlady was a little hard of hearing and did not like to use the phone.

Fourteen side plates, eight dinner plates, thirty-five glasses, one pottery vase, one case of beer, fifteen brand-new bottles of whiskey, four panes of glass from a china cabinet, one lightbulb . . . The landlady and Miss Sasaki sighed in what was almost admiration as they read the list of damages sent by the restaurant.

"Where on earth did that skinny old blockhead get that kind of strength?"

"It must have been the liveliest night he's had in a long time."

They discussed whether the amount calculated by the restaurant was exorbitant, but in the end, they decided he was lucky to get an out-of-court settlement at all, and the only course of action was to leave it in the hands of a friend of the landlady's who was a lawyer. Yet even after they had agreed on this, they still continued to pore over the list.

The landlady even visited the taxi company. Although they had turned a cold shoulder to Mr. Nishioka, she went repeatedly, taking gift boxes of sweets and begging them not to fire him. The president of the company, who was actually looking for any excuse to reduce his staff, must have met his match in this old woman who came every day despite the cold weather, dressed in her ancient kimono and leaving the pungent scent of camphor in her wake.

After listening to my rather tongue-tied explanation of the situation, my mother took a compote of sweet potatoes stewed with lemon to the landlady in the evening to see how she was doing. Mr. Nishioka happened to be there. At the end of the dark corridor we could catch a glimpse of him as he sat at the *kotatsu*, looking utterly crestfallen. My mother and I gave the landlady the compote at the front door and were about to leave when Miss Sasaki happened to pass the open doorway on her way home from work. Unaware that Mr. Nishioka was there, she stepped into the entranceway and began talking to the landlady. "Did you go to the taxi company again today? How about that blockhead's job? Are they going to keep him on?" But when Mr. Nishioka appeared and said, "I'm sorry to have caused you so much trouble," she bobbed her head in greeting, mumbling, "Oh, you're here."

"Yes, um, and thanks to you and Mrs. Yanagi I was able to keep my job."

"Well, that's great news," she said, without even a smile, and then she turned her back on the rest of us and dashed up the stairs as we squirmed uncomfortably. She came back with two big bottles of beer in each hand. "After all, it is certainly something to celebrate. Let's have a drink together."

That night the party lasted until quite late in the landlady's living room. In the three years I lived in Poplar House, that was the first and last time all the residents gathered to drink beer. After just half a glass, the landlady, hiccuping all the while, perhaps because the alcohol had gone to her head, began to rummage about in the closet, finally pulling out some ancient crackers that she had stored away. Miss Sasaki and my mother poured beer for each other, protesting that they couldn't possibly manage another drop, yet steadily increasing the speed with which they drank. Mr. Nishioka picked up an old Japanese lute called a *biwa*, though I can't imagine where he found it, and began plucking it in a melancholy fashion, then suddenly began to groan and burst into tears.

"Oh my," Miss Sasaki said with a small sigh. My mother stared at Mr. Nishioka, her hand still holding the glass frozen in midair. The landlady began to console him, saying, "It's been hard, I know, but—" when she was interrupted by another attack of the hiccups. And I just sat there not knowing what to do with the cracker I had already popped in my mouth.

Mr. Nishioka sat with head bowed, weeping in broken sobs, then suddenly he stood up. His face was bright red. His shoulders were shaking violently. Miss Sasaki, my mother, myself, and even the landlady, who was usually stooped over, sat up very straight.

"Mr. Nishioka . . ." my mother said, casting anxious glances at Miss Sasaki and the landlady.

"Listen, why don't you sit down. Drinking standing up will make you drunk faster," Miss Sasaki said. But whether he was listening or not, he took a large step forward and immediately caught his foot in the *kotatsu* quilt. His body, which looked like a scarecrow, swayed dangerously. He managed to right himself somehow, and with very jerky steps he went to the kitchen sink and gave the faucet a fierce twist. I thought he was going to wash his face, but instead he filled a cup with water and came back.

"Hiccups. Drink water. It helps."

The landlady reverently took the cup he proffered, although her hiccups already seemed to have stopped from her being so startled.

I don't know how many times Miss Sasaki went back and forth between her room and the landlady's bringing more beer. Pressured by a drunken Miss Sasaki, Mr. Nishioka performed a *rakugo* monologue called "Kaen-Daiko." Although my mother was the only one who laughed, he seemed very pleased, and repeated a line that seemed to mean something like "Don't be so shocked that you pee your pants" over and over to himself between sips of beer. Before I knew it, I had crawled inside the *kotatsu* quilt and fallen asleep while listening to the landlady sing a popular Japanese folk song in a tedious monotone that made it sound like a pilgrim's chant.

❧

As the days passed, small green leaves appeared on the naked branches of the poplar tree. The scent of grass and trees that tickled far back in my nose grew stronger daily. A stray cat had had kittens behind the shed. The mother cat bared her fangs and would not let anyone close, but every day I placed a saucer of milk out near the shed.

I was going through a rebellious period at the time. When I watched my mother's back as she worked in the kitchen, I was filled with an intense irritation, convinced that she had not opened her heart to me, that there was something she should have told me but as yet had not. I latched on to the most trifling, insignificant things—her brusqueness when saying good night, or her preoccupation with a TV show when she was supposedly listening to me—and grizzled at her. Child though I still was, I seemed to be spoiling for a fight. But the more I behaved like this, the less hold I seemed to have on my mother's heart, and I was stricken with a guilty conscience. I had stopped writing to my father. Having lost control of my own self, I did not have the means to put my frustration into words, nor did I even know if it was acceptable to do so.

It came as a great surprise to me, therefore, when my mother handed me an envelope.

"This is a letter to your father. You said that someone would take it to him if I wrote it, right?"

I remembered the night I had talked with her, New Year's Eve at my uncle's. "Yes, that's right."

"Could you give it to that person, then?"

I nodded and took the letter. On the smooth, cream-colored envelope the words "Mr. Shunzo Hoshino, from Tsukasa" were written in my mother's script. It had enough weight to rest firmly on the palm of my hand, and of course it was sealed shut.

I was glad my mother had accepted my offer. The next day I went straight to the landlady's when I got home from school and gave her the letter, which I had carefully packed in my schoolbag.

"I didn't break my promise to keep it a secret. I never said that it was you."

"Well, I suppose it's all right," she said and took the letter. "But you'll have to weed the yard in payment."

What was my mother thinking when she gave me that letter to my father? Did she really have something to say to him, or was she merely trying to placate me because I was complaining all the time? Whatever the case, after that my irritation with her subsided as if it had never been.

When spring vacation came, I spent my days chasing after the kittens in the landlady's yard. The landlady and I often weeded together. We each had a bag and we would compete to see who could fill hers first. On the black earth, which had been covered in frost during the winter, weeds that I had never seen before were springing up everywhere. Progress was slow because I frequently had to check with her. "Should I pull up this one?" I would ask, and she would say, "That's a violet," or "That's peppermint." But every so often she would sneak some of the weeds from her bag into mine. My shoes were now size six, and my mother bought me a sky blue skirt to start off the coming term as a replacement for the red skirt that was now too small. The manholes of which I had once been so afraid had vanished, and I had almost forgotten about their existence.

It was a gusty day in early April. "Don't open the window or the dust will fly in," my mother had said, and so I sat watching the poplar tree through the windowpane as it stood stolidly in the wind, while each gust seemed about to snatch off its newly acquired leaves. Sometimes the wind would hit the window where I sat with my nose pressed absently against the glass and startle me out of my daydreaming.

Gray clouds raced across the sky. I glanced down and noticed the landlady in the yard. Her white hair, whipped by the wind, was standing on end, and her legs, encased in several layers of socks that peeped out from under her tube-shaped skirt, were thrust against the ground as if declaring, I will not be conquered by the wind. What on earth could she be doing outside on a day like this? I wondered.

It didn't take me long to identify her objective. A rubber tree in a planter that she had left outside by the laundry rack had been overturned by the wind. She walked unsteadily toward it as though wading through water, putting all her strength in her stooped back, and righted the huge planter. Then, turning her rear end toward the sliding glass door, she began pulling the planter inch by inch, ever so patiently. If she is planning to get that thing into the house, I'd better go help, I thought. But just as I turned away from the window, the wind seemed to roll itself into a huge mass and howl. Startled, I turned once more to look below and saw that the landlady's back, which had been rigid with strain, was motionless. She had fallen over, her arms clasped around the rubber tree.

Unfortunately, both Miss Sasaki and Mr. Nishioka were out. I ran into the yard. While the wind raged violently and the dog on the corner barked as though it had gone mad, the space around the landlady seemed deathly silent. I ran, crying, to the neighbor's house and knocked on the door.

On my mother's day off from work, I accompanied her to the hospital to visit the landlady. It was, I believe, about three days after she had fallen. She wore an oxygen mask and lay sleeping. Her eyes, which always glared out at the world around her from beneath the hair on her broad overhanging forehead, were closed, and the white bedcovers looked flat. She seemed to have suddenly grown much smaller. I was shocked at her pitiful appearance. In contrast to the shock I had received when she was knocked over by the wind, this was like something cold and clammy seeping into me.

"Will she die?" I asked my mother on the way home from the hospital.

"She'll be fine," my mother answered, but as I had suspected, she was uneasy. Once again I saw the manhole, waiting for me with its gaping black maw. "Go away. I don't like you," I whispered, but it only laughed uncannily.

That evening my mother unlocked the door to the landlady's house. She and Miss Sasaki had decided to take turns on their days off bringing Mrs. Yanagi a change of pajamas and other things. My mother was to give the key to Miss Sasaki but had decided to get some clean underwear for the landlady and drop by the hospital on her way to work the next morning.

As I listened to my mother's footsteps descend the apartment stairs outside, I was thinking about that drawer. Didn't the sight of the landlady lying like a broken wooden doll prove that the drawer was at last full? But there was still something I could do to save her. And if I was going to do it before she was pulled into that black hole, my only chance was now, while the door was unlocked.

Stealthily I crept down the stairs after my mother. Fortunately, the front door was open and she was rummaging in the storage room across from the landlady's bedroom. Taking a chance, I tiptoed past and slipped into the familiar living room. I could hear my mother humming. She hadn't noticed me.

I brought a stool from the kitchen, placed it in front of the black chest of drawers, and stood on top. It was high enough that if I stretched I would just be able to see inside the top drawer. So now all I had to do was look. After all, hadn't the landlady told me that whoever looked inside would be the one to take the letters to the next world?

I certainly had no heroic thought of dying in her stead. It was merely that in some corner of my brain I had the desperate idea that if I just looked in that drawer, I could conquer my fear of being sucked into an open manhole. I simply couldn't bear the thought of the landlady dying. I wanted her to live.

I stepped purposefully onto the top of the stool and with all my strength pulled on the handles. The heavy drawer slid open with a surprisingly smooth and soundless motion. A pleasant fragrance like incense wafted upward and unconsciously I closed my eyes. I stretched onto my tiptoes. Now, I thought, open your eyes. Then the landlady will not have to die. Quickly, open your eyes.

But my eyes stayed firmly shut and the tips of my toes began to quake.

"What are you doing?" Startled by the unexpected

voice, I turned and met my mother's eyes. It could only have been a minute. I was so intent that I had completely forgotten she was there at all, and I was shocked to see her.

"What do you think you're doing? Looking in someone's dresser without permission!" My mother pushed the drawer with one hand and it clicked shut as if drawn by a magnet. I leaped off the stool with a thump. It was over. My mother would give the key to Miss Sasaki that night. My chance receded into the distance because I had not opened my eyes immediately.

That night I wrote to my father. It made no difference now whether I would give it to the landlady or not. But I wanted someone to save her, and if I was going to ask someone, then my father, rather than Jesus or anyone else, was who it would be. Strangely enough, while I was writing the letter, it was glimpses of my father, snatches of his voice, not the landlady's, that kept floating into my mind and vanishing again: my father eating quietly; the way he closed the door when he went out; the way he called "I'm home" when he returned; his hands as they moved to take off his coat, to which clung the chill air and the smell of cigarette smoke; his voice when he said my name.

I put the letter under my pillow and lay down. But the instant I did so, I knew that I could not possibly sleep. I deeply regretted the fear that had prevented me from looking in the drawer that afternoon, and I felt terribly ashamed.

I was still wide awake in the middle of the night when

the fresh light of the moon shone into the room. My mother was breathing peacefully on her futon. I felt like the only person in the whole world who was still awake, and before I knew it my pillow was hot and damp. The same thought ran through my head repeatedly as I rolled over; if only I could turn back the clock to the moment I had opened the drawer, this time I would look inside properly without any hesitation.

Just then the phone rang. The volume was turned down low, and my mother must have been very tired, for she did not budge. I got up, went into the kitchen, and picked up the receiver. I couldn't hear any voice—only a dry sound like the wind or like a long-distance phone call from somewhere very far away.

Before I had a chance to think, I said, "Father?" Perhaps it sounded like the static on the phone line when my father had called, so long ago, from England. *Tsu-tsu-tsu.* A different noise came on the line and then the phone went dead. I replaced the receiver and stood for a while, staring vacantly. The sound was still buzzing in my ear.

Then, quietly, from the very depths of my being, a sense of certainty rose within me. The landlady was going to be all right. That phone call must have been from my father in answer to my letter begging him to help. "Something amazing" had finally happened, that event for which I had been waiting so long. The fruit on the altar still rotted, but my father really was watching over me.

I believed this without a trace of doubt. The light of the moon, which just before had appeared to me to be shining without mercy, now seemed to pour down gently and familiarly, as if sharing a secret with a friend. And the poplar tree, which knew everything from beginning to end, was a most reliable witness. I returned to my futon on tiptoe, my former bitter regrets completely forgotten, and fell fast asleep.

That phone call might just have been a wrong number or a prank, I often thought to myself afterward. But even if that were true, it didn't matter, because it was possible for me to believe that it was my father. I felt serene in the knowledge that I, who had found the puzzle piece at last, would never again lose sight of him.

The landlady exhibited astonishing powers of recovery for a woman of her years, and one week after the phone call she was sitting up in bed and eating *mamedaifuku* that I had bought for her from the Nishikawa shop. I stopped in at the hospital to see her every day on my way home from school. I just had to get another look at this "something amazing" which had occurred right before my very eyes.

She was discharged from the hospital on a weekend in May. After she was driven home in Mr. Nishioka's taxi, the first thing she did was to stand gazing up at the poplar tree, its green leaves waving against the wide blue sky, blinking her eyes in the brightness. She snorted loudly—"hunh, hunh"—through her nose and then entered the house, prayed before her husband's picture on the altar, and slowly looked around the room. Now that she was installed back in the living room, the dragon sculpture I had once found so spooky, the old books, the yellowed wall hanging, all seemed surprisingly suited to this space.

A futon had been spread out in the same place where I had lain when I was ill. My mother and Miss Sasaki had probably put it there because the room had a television and it was bigger than the room where the landlady usually slept. My mother had told me, "When she has changed and gone to bed, you come right home." It was doubtless my mother and Miss Sasaki again who had decided that it was better to leave me there than to have an adult fussing over the landlady.

But she took her time about going to bed. She went to the kitchen and opened the cupboard doors instead, rummaged in a little drawer under the altar and pulled out an old nail file, patted the back of a legless chair, and muttered to herself. I watched her a little anxiously.

She stretched out her arm and ran a finger along the top of the black chest of drawers. Then she turned and, leaning forward to peer at me, her forehead slightly paler since her stay in the hospital, she caught my eyes where I sat on the tatami. I could feel my face growing redder and redder as she looked at me. It seemed that her gaze could penetrate everything. But then she slid her eyes away from mine and began to change her clothes. Feeling that it was rude to stare at her while she was undressing, I was looking down when she said to me, "That drawer isn't full yet, you know. Unfortunately, I have to keep living."

"Really?" I raised my face abruptly. She towered above me, now wearing her pale pink short-sleeved undershirt and knee-length underwear.

"Really," she said. I had expected her to change into her pajamas, but instead she was putting on the gray tube-shaped skirt she usually wore around the house.

"How much is 'not full yet'?"

"Hmm, well, not full yet is, you know, just not full yet."

"Not until I grow up?"

"Now, that sure is a long time in the future." And she did not reply any further. She began slowly buttoning a familiar russet cardigan, one button at a time from the top down. Then the two of us ate some instant sweet-bean soup that was left in the cupboard.

"Ah, that's better. It's so nice to be in my own home doing what I want. I can sleep when I like, get up when I like, and eat whatever I like." She crinkled her already wrinkled face as she ate the floury soup. But I was still far from feeling carefree. She took a long look at my dejected face and then said, "You didn't peek in that drawer, did you?"

I wished that I could say yes, but I could not tell a lie. "I tried, but I couldn't open my eyes."

When she heard that, she began to laugh. And she laughed and laughed for what seemed like forever, her back hunched over as though it were so funny she could not help herself. What with embarrassment and anger, I wished that I could vanish from the spot. And she had caused me so much worry. Well, next time, see if I gave a hoot.

But then she said to me, "Just the thought of still being alive when you grow up makes me shudder. But, well, I suppose I can try."

A May breeze entered through the open window. She closed her eyes as though listening to the sound of the rustling poplar leaves.

*Father,*

*How are you? The landlady came back from the hospital today. She touched everything in her house and looked very happy. It was a problem because she wouldn't go to bed even though she is supposed to rest still. But when she did go to bed, she taught me a special charm for sleeping. It goes like this:*

*Neru yori rakuwa nakarikeri*
*ukiyo no bakawa okite hataraku.*
(Sleeping is the easiest thing in the world,
But foolish men stay up and work.)

*She told me that the reason she got better so fast is because she always chants this charm before she goes to sleep. I told her about you, too. I told her that when I prayed to you for her to be cured, you phoned me, and she said, "Then I will have to tell him how much I appreciate it."*

*I went to church in the evening. The other day I found a pretty gold cigarette lighter, although it doesn't work, and I went to give it to Jesus. But in just the short time since I saw him last, he stopped looking like you at all. I asked him, "What happened to you? That's no good." He looked like someone who feels carsick and he didn't say anything.*

*Instead, these days I often think of you. It seems strange when not long ago I couldn't remember you at all. I know you cannot be with the rabbit on the moon, and I am sure you are not a sheep, either. I think you are somewhere quietly smoking, reading, and working, just like you did before.*

*I want to call you, but I don't know your phone*

number, so instead I dial the weather recording. Listening to the weather forecast is fun. And sometimes I think, It probably costs a lot of money to make a phone call from where my father is now. He can't call me unless it is something very special like last time.

Yesterday Noriko Hashiguchi felt sick in class, so I took her to the nurse's room. I'm the person in charge of taking people to the nurse for our class. Noriko and I were the only people walking down the hall. I was very worried. Then I heard a song coming from the music room. It was one you used to listen to. I stopped feeling so worried. I said to Noriko, "It's okay. You can throw up if you want." She looked a bit surprised and then she said, "Thank you, Chiaki." She told me she ate doughnuts for breakfast. Her mother told her, "Doughnuts are too greasy. Save them for your snack when you get home." But she ate them anyway. That's why she felt sick. She was worried that her little brother would eat them while she was at school. "I should have shared them with him later," she said. I thought I would like to be friends with her. I was glad I was the person in charge of taking people to the nurse.

I am going to stop writing to you for a while. Because if I write, I will take up all the space in the landlady's drawer. I don't think that would be fair because her job is to deliver letters from many people. And besides, I will be okay because I know that you are watching over me.

From now on, I will write to you in my heart. I will write much more than I have before. And if you are still lonely, please call me again. Even late at night is okay.

Goodbye for now.

## Chapter 10

A S I TURN THE CORNER at the fire station and begin walking along the road by the creek, for a fraction of a second I am overcome by the illusion that I have never left this place. The same fragrance I used to smell is in the air. Although a large shopping center now stands in front of the station and the street has been greatly altered, the Nishikawa shop still sells the landlady's favorite *mamedaifuku*, and so I stop and buy some.

The creek is bathed in the clear autumn light, and my silhouette, with its sharp shoulders that make my mother exclaim, "You're too thin!" every time I see her, is reflected distinctly in the water's surface. I wonder if the water, which was frequently frothy with soapsuds when I was a child, is any cleaner now.

It was just such an autumn day when the landlady first told me about the letters to the next world. How like her to do such a thing, I realize, and what a perfect way to cheer up a six- or seven-year-old child. No one can deny that it was because I wrote those letters that I was able to break free of the anxiety which gripped me, or that I was able to believe a silent phone call in the middle of the night was from my father. Moreover, she kept every letter I wrote, and they must have amounted to quite a number.

If only I could, I would like to tell her, "It's thanks to you that I am now so happy." But as soon as this thought occurs to me, I am overcome by that familiar, despised tightening in my chest and I stop in my tracks.

What have I done to myself? I fell in love with a silent man whose thoughts I found unfathomable. He was a technician in the hospital where I worked. And he was always quiet, like a child who has become accustomed to playing on his own. In time, he began to come to my apartment, and as long as I didn't ask him questions like "When will you come again?" he would usually nod submissively at whatever I said.

It's ridiculous to fall in love with someone you cannot understand. But I felt at ease when I was with him, though he was a man who seemed shut within a hard shell. I was much more uncomfortable with eloquent and easy talkers;

although somewhere inside I felt a deep yearning for their company, they made me feel timid and afraid.

Perhaps there is a connection between this aspect of my character and my image of my father. The loneliness I felt at not being able to penetrate his silence and his warmth that eased this emptiness are inseparably linked inside me. Perhaps I am unable to feel tenderness or warmth without experiencing that quiet loneliness I felt with my father.

Recently, when I think of him, I am filled with a kind of bitterness. He should have spoken to me more. Then I would not have been starved for words, attracted by and then afraid of them. But it is a useless accusation, although it may not be entirely unjustified. Trying to explain the sum of my life this year by dragging in a man who died almost twenty years ago is like claiming that the only thing I was bequeathed at birth was a silent father who died young.

Yes, it is ridiculous to blame my father. "I should just forget about it," I chide myself. "Accept the fact that you were blind. That's all." But no matter how I try to convince myself, I am haunted by the same dream. I am being carried, crying, into the operating room. "I'm sorry, but it is too late," the doctor says, looking into my face and injecting the anesthetic while ordering me to repeat after him, "One. Two. Three . . ." As he chants the numbers, his face becomes that of the other man. "Can't we talk about marriage another time? Surely it was fate that you miscarried." That was all he had said. I would rather he had remained silent, saying nothing, than to hear those words.

I quit my job at the hospital partly because it was painful to be in the same workplace as my lover, but if that had been the only reason, I could have just switched to a different hospital. I had, in fact, lost confidence in myself as a nurse. The winds of fear had blown upon me. My only desire was to distance myself as far as possible from the terrifying and ghastly memory of lying as a patient on the operating table, and I tucked my tail between my legs and ran.

The paper bag full of medicine is still in the small overnight bag I carry in my right hand. If it comes to that, I can drink the whole lot: this thought is constantly in my mind, and the fact that I have not yet done so is because I am a coward. Yet oddly enough, the knowledge that I still have the option of taking an overdose gives me the feeling that I can go on for one more day, just one more day. For the last few weeks I have somehow managed with the vision of taking the drugs as my only future, as though saving something special to enjoy for the end. That is, if you can call this a future.

It is time to stop pretending. Like someone in a strange country left behind at a crowded ticket counter for long-distance passenger trains, I am nervous and impatient. I must hurry, hurry, and decide my destination. But where on earth should I go?

Just then I raise my face, and there is the poplar tree, bathed in the afternoon sunlight, its golden leaves faintly rustling. It is neither past nor future, dream nor counterfeit. It is so much a solid reality that for an instant my mind goes totally blank. The poplar never bothers to think that it has no place to go. It simply is where it is now. And I, too, I am here now.

I draw a deep breath and begin to walk again, staring at the beckoning poplar tree, just as I had on the first day I came.

"Chiaki? It is you, isn't it? Welcome!" Miss Sasaki greets me with a cheerfulness that makes it hard to believe anyone has died, despite the mourning clothes she wears for appearances' sake.

"Miss Sasaki. It's been a long time."

"Yes, it really has. You've grown up, haven't you? But I recognized you right away."

She must be fifty by now, but her hair is still bobbed the way it used to be, and although she has a few crow's-feet around her eyes, her skin, unadorned by makeup as usual, is fresh.

"Hasn't changed, has it, this place?"

"No, not at all."

The gate, the yard, the shadowy dimness of the entrance hall, and this smell, everything is just as it was. Except that, judging by the number of shoes overflowing from the entranceway, there seems to be a surprisingly large crowd of people inside.

The timid-looking, white-bearded old man that the landlady had called her Professor had left his wife and children when he was young and run off with Mrs. Yanagi, who was then an elementary school teacher. They never had children, and ever since they eloped, his connection with his relations had been severed. I had learned this when the landlady was blown over by the wind, and so I had simply assumed that it would be a quiet funeral.

As I stand at the door, stunned, Miss Sasaki says, "Hurry up and come inside. They're all your comrades."

What does she mean, "my comrades"? I wonder dubiously as I enter to find the house jammed with people. Men and women are sitting, talking, in the room next to the front door that she had used as a bedroom, in the living room, and even in the kitchen. The majority of them, both male and female, are elderly. Not one of them exhibits the fidgeting or stiff expressions that are common in such situations. No one is weeping or wailing either. The doors and windows are opened wide and everything is dyed with the golden light that floods into the room through the yellow leaves of the poplar tree. Everyone just sits there, drinking tea and looking very relaxed.

In the living room, across from the familiar black dresser, a small altar has been set up by the bookcase built into the wall, and in front of it lies the landlady's coffin. Having placed an envelope of money and the *mamedaifuku* as offerings at the altar, I bend over to see her face. As I look through the small window in the coffin, a man comes over and lifts the coffin lid for me. A familiar, pleasant aroma rises from inside. It is the same smell as when I had opened the drawer.

"Oh!" I catch my breath in wonder.

"It's amazing, isn't it? Unbelievable." The man who opened the lid is smiling broadly. He is about sixty, with fluffy white hair that has been brushed back off his forehead and a round, refined face. "I was astounded. It never occurred to me that there would be so many."

The landlady lies in the coffin, wrapped in a beautiful light purple kimono, and surrounded by hundreds of letters. The man gently spreads the palm of his hand over her feet. "I took the liberty of placing mine in this area."

"You mean . . ." I hesitate, unable to finish the question with the words "you, too?"

"Yes, that's right." He nods his round head, reminiscent of a full moon, bashfully, like an awkward little boy. "I'm sorry. I forgot to introduce myself. I'm Yamane from the Yamashina Funeral Parlor."

As for me, I am struck dumb with surprise, for I had been convinced that this tale of delivering letters to the next world was simply something the landlady had made up for my sake when I was a child.

Her face has become very, very small, but her broad forehead, so dear to my heart, is just as I remembered it. Her eyes are closed and the corners of her single line of a mouth seem to be slightly upturned, as though she is laughing a little. She sleeps, her face like that of an evil Popeye during infancy. As I stare at her, my tears suddenly begin to overflow. It is true that after my mother remarried we moved far away, but still, why didn't I come to see her? After I grew up, I could have come to see her any time I wanted.

"Here. These are yours."

Miss Sasaki plops a thick wad of letters into my hand. The words "To Father, from Chiaki," written in the childish script of my younger years, leap out at me. Most of the envelopes are cheap brown ones, but the one on top was a freebie that came with a magazine and it has pictures of narcissi on it. I can still see traces where I rubbed out part of my name with an eraser and rewrote it.

Feeling rather giddy, I bend over to place the bundle of envelopes at the landlady's feet, but Mr. Yamane gently restrains my hand and, taking the bundle, places it just below her breast. Then, with graceful movements, he quietly closes the coffin lid.

"I first met Mrs. Yanagi," he begins as he sips the tea Miss Sasaki poured for him, "at a funeral. The deceased was a student of her husband. He was a scholar, and when there was trouble over payment of the funeral costs, well, Mrs. Yanagi asked me to come and see her and started telling me about the letters. She said that when she died, she would deliver letters for me to someone in the next world, and so I should reduce the fee. It was crazy."

"And then I bet she told you the story about her cousin who died when she was a child," I interject.

But he replies, "No, not her cousin. It was her dead sister. It was a good story." He smiles slightly at my perplexed expression and continues. "At first I was disgusted. I had just lost my only son in an accident, and I couldn't help despising my work. You would think that, having suffered myself, I would have had more compassion for other people's pain, but I was afraid to. I told my co-workers that the deceased were just commercial goods and took perverse pleasure in being frowned upon. It was despicable, but that's how I was.

"So I wrote a letter. Somehow she inspired me to do it, and in return, instead of reducing the fees, I did the entire funeral for free. And I began writing straight through from the evening of the same day. I wrote all the things I wanted to say to my son, I told him I was sorry, and demanded to know whether he could understand just how painful his death was for a parent, about the plans I'd had for doing things with him. I'll tell you what hurts most. It's being able to see the future. I wrote about the future that might have been had he lived, the future that I could still see no matter how many times I tried to wipe it away, and the anger that would not die. I wrote and wrote, and when I had finished, I brought the bulging envelope here and gave it to Mrs. Yanagi. But within less than three days, I began to suffer again, and stayed up all night writing, bringing another letter the next day. I don't know how many times I repeated that process. But one day, I heard a voice saying, 'It's all right now. It's all right, you don't have to suffer anymore.' " He looks down and his mouth tightens into a single line. Then he says, "The people who have gathered here today, they are all people who entrusted letters to Mrs. Yanagi. All of them were helped by her."

As if drawn by him, I look around. All these people who are sitting here now, talking comfortably with one another—did the landlady really approach each one of them? Did she really reach out to them, one by one, as she found them, perhaps weeping or staring vacantly, perhaps wearing a stiff, strained expression or too anxious to show any expression at all; people who could no longer lend an ear even to the sobs of a child in distress or those who were afraid; on the street or in the doctor's waiting room, at the Nishikawa shop or on the train, at someone's funeral or on a park bench; on the roof of a department store or on a bridge?

A gust of wind sways the branches of the poplar. The yellow leaves dance upward and the golden light pouring down moves with them.

"You mentioned earlier that she told you about her cousin who had died." I can hear a sigh mixed with the slightest hint of mischief in Mr. Yamane's voice.

I nod in assent. "And she told you about a sister?"

"Yes, she did. She told everyone a different story."

"Everyone?"

"Yes. It seems that in every case she started out by telling her own story, but the actual content was different each time. The person who died was her father, a girl the same age as herself, even her younger brother, who was able to read at the age of three months."

"Really?"

"I've been here since yesterday, and have asked many different people, but not one of the stories is the same. I keep thinking that maybe, just maybe you understand, whatever happened to Mrs. Yanagi was too painful for her to tell the truth."

I wonder whether this could be the case, but Mr. Yamane, who has been looking down, raises his face and says, "But, you know, it's quite useless to speculate about things like that. And besides, knowing her, she might just as likely have enjoyed making up stories and convincing people they were true. I mean, don't you suppose that was just the sort of person she was?"

In my mind, the landlady grins as if to say, "Look at this dim-witted undertaker talking nonsense."

"Yes, I think so, too. I certainly wouldn't put it past her," I respond. He smiles as if relieved at my answer, the skin around his eyes crinkling up.

As it grows darker, even more people arrive. Miss Sasaki and I telephone the sushi shop and the liquor store several times to order deliveries. We cook rice and make rice balls, pour tea, and generally work very hard. Of course, the elderly women, who up until this time have been leisurely sipping tea, are much more seasoned campaigners than I or Miss Sasaki, and they don freshly starched white aprons or elegant black mourning aprons with lace trim they have brought with them, almost as if they are saying, "Now, let's get to it," working in unison like a team that has been together for decades and completing every task with great efficiency. Miss Sasaki, astounded, exclaims, "We can't compete with them," and she hands me the landlady's big black handbag, making me responsible for accounting, and appoints herself responsible for provisions, obeying the commands of these worthy superiors, running back and forth between the supermarket and Poplar House to replenish supplies of pickles, seaweed, fruit, tea, toilet paper, and anything else that is needed.

When the chanting of the Buddhist prayers for the wake is finished, we set up a folding table supplied by Mr. Yamane in the yard, because the house is just too small. The kerosene heater placed out by the laundry rack glows red, and the table is spread with a feast of sushi, fried chicken, pickles, and rice balls. Miss Sasaki and I travel back and forth between the kitchen and the yard, serving sake mulled by an old man who has "lived on this street for forty years." He is a small man who only reaches as high as my shoulder, and either because he has drunk a lot of sake or because he has just come from a hot bath, his skin is glowing. His gaze as he watches the sake bottles bobbing in the pot of warm water is like that of a grandfather fondly watching over his grandchildren in the bath. He worked for years warming sake in a restaurant and is apparently capable of judging by the number of guests, the type of gathering, and the menu the exact timing required to obtain the perfect temperature, not too hot, of mulled sake. I curse the clumsiness of my fingers in serving it, but everyone comments on how good it is. "This sake is really very delicious, isn't it?"

The guests, now sufficiently warmed, begin to leave by threes and fives beneath the starlit sky. The ten or so elderly people who remain behind to help clean up clearly intend to stay with Mrs. Yanagi all night. Some of them, however, have already been here from the previous day, so Miss Sasaki and I spread out rented futons with rather gaudy patterns in the empty rooms on the second floor. Miss Sasaki is the only tenant living here now.

The apartment where my mother and I had once lived, far from being familiar, comes as rather a surprise. Could we really have lived in such a small space with such a low ceiling? But when I rattle open the storm windows, there is the poplar tree gazing in at me as usual, and then I, too, begin to see. Me, perching my small rump on the ledge of the windowsill, and my mother sitting at the table, writing.

"This apartment was vacated about two years ago. It was old and nobody would live in it if it was left just like that. Then last year, when the one next door—yes, you're right, Mr. Nishioka lived there then, you remember well—when the tenant moved out, the landlady said she didn't feel like renting it again. I wonder if she knew." Miss Sasaki tells me these things as she struggles to smooth the stiffly starched sheets with her hands to spread them out. "You know, this entire place is going to be donated to some society for the study of Chinese literature that helped Mr. Yanagi a long time ago. The landlady was really pleased because they are going to make an award in his name."

Then she mutters almost to herself, "I'll never be able to

find such a comfortable place to live, that's for sure. I'm thinking I'd rather go back to my hometown." Her hands move even more busily as she says this.

In the middle of the night, when there is a lull in our work, Miss Sasaki and I pour ourselves some hot tea and eat the *mamedaifuku*. The other guests must have been tired, for most of them are asleep on the futons still wearing their clothes. The only people left by the landlady's coffin are two old men, who until recently were talking in low voices and whose heads are now nodding with sleep. Miss Sasaki and I sit across from one another at the kitchen table.

"Ah, that was a hard day's work. If you hadn't come, Chiaki, I don't know how on earth I would have managed." She finishes one of the sweets, drinks her tea to the last drop, and then lights a cigarette. "At this rate, the funeral tomorrow is going to be even worse."

"Was it you who contacted all these people?"

"It wasn't as if she asked me to, but she had done a lot for me, and I thought maybe I should go all out. She had kept a written record, you know, like an address book, about the people who had given her letters."

"Really?"

"It's amazing. She wrote down the date she received each one and in the column under 'Comments' she wrote things like 'One new salted salmon' or 'One wool blanket.'

Those must be the things she received in exchange. She was quite sharp."

"Did you," I ask after some hesitation, "give her a letter, too?"

She shakes her head and presses the burning tip of her half-smoked cigarette into the ashtray. "The first time I heard about it was half a year ago, I think. I was really taken aback. After all, it sounds quite zany. 'When I die,' she said to me, 'I want you to dress me in this kimono and place all the letters in this drawer in my coffin.' Then she gave me a very large jade necklace. I told her I didn't need it, but she said, 'If I give it to you, then you will feel obliged to do something in return.' She had a lot of nerve, didn't she?"

She goes on to tell me in a little more detail about the period before the landlady's death. She looked after herself and was quite healthy until the end, but gradually she lost her appetite until finally all she was eating was pickled plums and beans. In the last two or three years her eyesight had failed her, and she was no longer able to read the newspaper, a pastime she had so greatly enjoyed. I find the saddest thing for me is that she always said, "A person's life is over when they allow themselves to become grubby. It's a sign that they will soon be coming to get you," and so, no matter how bothersome it might be, she had a bath every three days, and even when she was sick with a cold, she still scrubbed her body vigorously with hot water. Perhaps she was just attached to living, but I cannot help reproaching myself for not coming to see her when she had done her best to live a long life for me.

I was ten when my mother decided to remarry and we were to leave Poplar House. I think it was a few days before we moved, and I was unable to tell anyone my feelings, to say that I did not want to leave, when the landlady said to me, "You know that fat cat you always give milk to? I don't know what you see in that cat. It's got a great hulking body but it's a weakling in a fight. Its voice is hoarse, and it's greedy, too. But if you like that cat, then, no matter where you may go, that cat that you like is yours. As long as you never give up that whim which makes you say you love that disgraceful old cat."

"That's a funny picture, isn't it?" I raise my face at the sound of Miss Sasaki's voice. She is looking at the photograph of the landlady on the altar. "She had that taken herself. She put on a kimono and went all the way to the photo studio. She really didn't need to put her dentures in, though."

"But she was 'going out,' " I say, and the next instant we both burst out laughing. We hastily suppress our voices and look toward the coffin. The two old men are still asleep, but it seems to me that the landlady in the photograph looks annoyed.

"Chiaki, what are you doing these days? I'm still making animal costumes and princess dresses. That's all I do."

As she presses me for answers, I tell her that I became a nurse but am currently unemployed.

"You quit, did you?"

"Yes, well . . ." I mumble vaguely, and she lights another cigarette.

"Your mother seemed well."

"Yes."

"Her voice on the phone hadn't changed a bit. That placid way she'd always had of talking. She remarried, didn't she?"

"Yes, right after we moved. My stepfather runs a construction firm."

We fall silent for a while. I always feel guilty when I think of my stepfather and my stepbrother and stepsister. They are good people, they are good to me, but I have always felt that I don't belong in their home.

One of the old men has been nodding back and forth, and suddenly his head hits the glass windowpane, making a loud noise. Miss Sasaki stands up and brings blankets from the next room. Saying, "It's gotten chilly, hasn't it?" she hands one to the old man, who is grinning in some embarrassment, and carefully wraps the other around the shoulders of the second man, whose head is buried in his chest as he sleeps. Then she opens a cupboard behind me and, from under a thick stack of new cloths, pulls out an envelope.

"Your mother asked me to tell you to read this."

My eyes are riveted on the envelope. That familiar handwriting. It is the letter, the only letter from my mother to my father, the one that I had given to the land-lady long ago.

"Yesterday I called your mother, and a little while after we hung up, she called me back."

"To tell you to give me this?"

"That's right."

So my mother knew that I had entrusted her letter to the landlady. What does she mean by telling me to read it? And why now?

Miss Sasaki pats me on the shoulder as I sit absently. "Why not ask Mr. Yamane to put it in the coffin for you tomorrow morning after you've read it?" Then she heads outside, saying that she is going upstairs to rest for a couple of hours. I sit stunned for several minutes with the cream-colored envelope in my hand. I have no idea what could be written there or how I should prepare myself to read it. This is the way my mother always does things. Just when I am convinced that she is not paying any attention to me, she suddenly turns to focus on me full force.

Knowing that although I may glare at the envelope, I have already lost the battle, I finally open the drawer above the cupboard, from which Miss Sasaki had taken the letter. Just as I had thought, the contents have not changed since my childhood. There are neatly coiled lengths of ribbon and string, and in a thin cookie box, along with some glue, a measuring tape, and cellophane tape, there is a pair of scissors. Feeling slightly calmer, I take those dull scissors in my hand and open my mother's letter.

## Chapter 11

*To Mr. Shunzo Hoshino:*

*Half a year has passed since you died. I sold the house, moved, and found a job. So many things must have happened in just that half year, yet when I look back, I feel like I slept right through it. As you well know, I tend to be rather dreamy and absentminded anyway, but recently I have become even more forgetful than usual. Just the other day I forgot to fix a torn seam on Chiaki's gym clothes, although she had asked me to do it some time ago. Poor Chiaki wore it torn for two weeks.*

*I am aware that my present state is the result of putting myself under too much strain. Yet, when I lower my guard even a fraction, I am swept up in a vicious circle of terrible remorse and endless self-*

reproach. "I should have had more compassion" or "If only I had spoken to you when you turned your back, everything would have been different"—ideas like these run through my mind.

I have even thought that if I could, I would wipe you from my memory. But the more I think along this line, the more anxious Chiaki becomes, and there is nothing I can do about that.

Possibly I have become slightly unbalanced. When I learned that Chiaki was secretly writing letters to you and, I suspected, taking them to the landlady, I went and complained. I told the landlady that she shouldn't encourage a child to do something that would only emotionally disturb and confuse her. I really let her have it.

But she simply led me, inflamed as I was with irrational anger, quietly into her room and let me read Chiaki's letters. In her letters, Chiaki is trying, somehow, to bring you whom she has lost back to her again with all the strength contained in her small frame and her child's soul. Regardless of the fact that the landlady was still in the room, I could not restrain myself from weeping at the thought of Chiaki's misery. More than that, however, I was made aware of an important fact that, as her mother, I cannot ignore.

*Chiaki is really very much like you. I became deeply aware of this as I read her letters. She is not like me, content to muddle heedlessly through life as long as the end results make some sort of sense. Chiaki will, without a doubt, come to realize that I have lied to her about your death, and that thought makes me quake.*

*As she matures, she will grow to resemble you even more. Like you, although silent, she will be sensitive to others' pain, and because she is sensitive, she will seek solitude, yet she will also feel compelled to be of service to others. That is the kind of person she will become. The difficult side of her character will also become more pronounced with time. And the more like you she becomes, the more she may yearn for you. That is, of course, if she lives at all.*

*I intend to continue telling her that you died in a car accident. It is perhaps only common sense to conceal a father's suicide from a small child, but I believe in this case I must guard this secret even more closely than that. I cannot get it out of my mind that if Chiaki were to learn that—despite the great height from which you leaped, your body appeared almost miraculously beautiful—she would be drawn toward the same course of action. Because, after all, she has inherited your same spirit.*

*Some may say that I am wasting my time. That it will make no difference whether she knows the facts or not; that, just as the moon draws the sea and the tide rolls in, the power of attraction that draws her heart is innate. Others, with knowing expressions, may even say that it is wrong to conceal the truth. How much better it would be for me, they might think, to bind her securely by telling her everything, by baring my heart to her, spilling out even my resentment toward you, and adding the admonition that the one thing she must never do, no matter what, is commit suicide . . . But I simply cannot do it. The burden would be too much for that child to bear, and if there is no guarantee that she will be safe no matter how forcefully I try to convince her, then there is only one course of action left open to me: to continue guarding this secret. Knowing her, she will become very frustrated with me and rebel. I am deeply concerned by this.*

*It is still too painful for me to write down my memories. I fill my heart with bitterness against you to protect myself from the grief, and I am as yet unable to remove this armor. You went and died without uttering a word, clutching your pain to yourself. You walked casually out the door, pretending things were just as usual, as if you were going for a walk just as you often did the day before you had to de-*

liver a difficult judgment in court. But then you wrote a letter to an old lover and committed suicide, despite the fact that you could not have been ignorant of how much suffering your actions would cause me.

The landlady told me that if I wrote a letter to you, I could bring it to her. She said that it is by entrusting the letter to a carrier, whether the postman or a bottle floating in the sea, that the heart of the writer is truly freed. Although it sounds like a childish trick, oddly enough, when she said it, I could feel the tightness that has gripped my heart loosen its hold, whether I willed it or not. I intend to ask Chiaki to take this letter to the landlady, but only because I know that it will please Chiaki.

I am sure that from this time on, I will write you many letters. I will probably be unable to stop myself from writing tens, perhaps hundreds of letters. And I intend to keep all those letters myself. I will think, over and over again, about why you had to die, sometimes reading the letters I have written, and I will always live with this question continuously in my mind. But that itself is the nature of the bond that joins me to you. When all is said and done, I cannot erase the bond that exists between us. If I can neither run away from it nor forget it, then there is nothing else for me to do.

When Chiaki has grown up and found her own

*way of life, when I can believe that she will be all
right, I want her to know the truth. By then I believe
that I will be ready to tell her everything, both the
joy and the sorrow.*

*Until then, please watch over her. Although I still
cannot yet completely accept what you have done, I
have surely already forgiven you, simply because of
the fact that I met you, loved you, and have been entrusted with Chiaki, whose heart and mind so closely
resemble yours.*

*Tsukasa*

I sit motionless, thinking. My father chose his death
himself. And that is all right. Sufficient time has passed.
And who was it that gave me that time? My mother.

Just as my mother had foreseen, my yearning for an ab-
sent father had swelled uncontrollably when I was in ju-
nior high school. My mother reprimanded me because my
grades had begun to fall, and I turned on her and snapped,
"What about your life? Don't you even feel sorry for Father?" That was the one and only time I ever said such a
thing.

My mother did not become angry or cry. Nor did she
fling the truth at me. All she did was say in a quiet, lonely,
and yet very clear voice, "You are so like him."

Later I asked her many times how I was like my father.

But she merely responded with "You have a difficult character" or "You're introverted. It's hard to know what you're thinking," which, though not lies, really did not seem to be important. No matter how I pressed, my mother just closed up. Although there are times when it is better to leave the things you don't understand alone, I could not do this. I deliberately interpreted my mother's words literally, convincing myself that my mother hated me because I was like my father.

Not only did this type of thinking give me a sweet sense of mission that I was the only one who could give my father comfort, but it also, in some way, made things easier for me. If I was shunned by my mother because I was like my father, then I could assure myself that there was no pretense in my mother's happiness in her second marriage, for my stepfather was a good man, lively and active, and his character was obviously, even at a single glance, completely different from my father's. My mother's natural optimism had been restored within this new family, yet my inability to accept my mother's choice, despite my stepfather's kindness, except in such a twisted manner, must have been due more than anything else to her secret. In the depths of my heart I clung to a single aspiration, stubborn to a mysterious degree. While on the one hand I yearned for my father, at the same time I wanted my mother to be enveloped in a happiness untouched by any trace of cloud, a happiness that was dazzling in its perfection. This desire was so strong and specific that at times it was almost painful.

"You are so like him."

When my mother said that, had she sealed away even her own sorrow? So as not to lose me, concentrating all her heart on that single objective? How strong then, too, was the desire that she had nurtured.

Perhaps my mother, recognizing that I was going through a time of pain, had thought, If I do not share this letter now, I will never be able to speak the truth for the rest of my life. Or does she really think that I have become a dependable adult and have no insecurities in life? Does she really believe that?

I wipe my wet cheeks repeatedly with my fingertips until they are completely dry. And as I do so, I begin to chuckle. If she really thinks that I have grown up, then she's wide of the mark. Honestly. My mother.

As I return the letter to the envelope and trace the feminine script with a finger, I whisper, "Thank you, Mother."

## Chapter 12

THE NEXT MORNING I hear several bursts of fireworks thundering in the clear sky as if in celebration of the landlady's funeral. There must be a sports event somewhere nearby. Many people who appear to have been students of her husband also arrive for the ceremony, and they spill out into the garden, where they listen to the chanting of the prayers. "Lovely weather, isn't it?" "Yes, it certainly is." "That long period of rain just a few days ago seems like it never happened now." "You're right." "My knees are bad, so if the weather wasn't as nice as this, I couldn't have left the house." "Me, too. Really, knowing Mrs. Yanagi, I bet she struck a bargain with Providence." I hear snatches of such conversations at intervals.

I listen to the prayers from beside the poplar tree. Between the sparse leaves I can see three faintly colored snake gourds and also a bird's nest. I pick up one of the fallen leaves and start to put it in my pocket, but stop immediately. If they tear down the apartment building, who knows what will happen to the poplar tree, but I know that I will never forget it, and that is enough.

When it is time for the hearse carrying the coffin to leave, I am quite surprised when I go out into the street. A huge, gleaming bus covered entirely with painted cherry blossoms is standing in the road along the creek.

"Please hurry and board the bus. I'm blocking the road, so please move along," the driver, wearing mourning clothes and white gloves, is calling out as he helps the elderly passengers onto the bus.

"Mr. Nishioka!"

"Er . . ."

"I'm Chiaki. Chiaki Hoshino."

"Ch-Chiaki?" He has gained a little weight and the white in his hair, which has receded even further, is prominent, but his timid-looking face and his unsteady tenor voice that so easily flips into falsetto hasn't changed a bit. "My, how you've grown! You've grown up!"

I had no expectation of meeting Mr. Nishioka here. He had moved out of Poplar House even before Mother and I, and for a particular reason, although I was really only guessing at that. About three months before he moved, he had asked Miss Sasaki as she was coming down the stairs, "W-would you like to g-g-go with me to see Shincho perform?" Miss Sasaki had refused point-blank, saying, "I'm not interested in *rakugo*." Listening from a playhouse made out of a cardboard box under the stairs, I could distinctly hear Mr. Nishioka's enormous sigh.

Mr. Nishioka is speaking, his eyebrows twitching as usual. He started a taxi business ten years ago with his friends, he tells me.

"But we aren't much yet. It would be nice if we could own a bus like this one, but I borrowed it. Miss Sasaki said to get the biggest one. And not too solemn, either." He pats the bus with his gloved hand.

Miss Sasaki closes the iron gate, which protests with a creaking sound, and runs toward us. "You can talk later! I'm going with Mrs. Yanagi, so you're responsible for the rest!" She leaps into the hearse.

"She's amazing," Mr. Nishioka mutters in admiration, watching the hearse depart. "For fifteen, no, sixteen years, we just sent each other postcards. Then suddenly she calls me, and look what we've got." He narrows his eyes, still gazing in the direction the hearse has gone. Then he lowers his voice so that the people still climbing onto the bus cannot overhear. "Chiaki, what relation are all these people to the landlady? Are they her relatives? Her friends?"

"Er, well, her friends."

"All of them?"

"Yes, all of them."

He nods to himself. "I always thought she was no ordinary person."

The bus heads for the crematorium located on top of the hill, bathed in the autumn sunlight. The seats are soft and they recline.

"This is great. So comfortable. It's like we're going to paradise, too," I hear the woman beside Mr. Yamane say excitedly. It feels to me as if we're going on a school excursion.

"How's Osamu?" I lean over the front seat to talk with Mr. Nishioka.

"He's fine, fine. But he's obsessed."

"How do you mean?"

"He's besotted with mountains."

"He climbs mountains?" I can't immediately picture the skinny Osamu as a mountaineer.

"Mmm. And he takes photos, too. Regardless of whether you can even earn money that way, it's dangerous. I keep telling him not to go alone, but he's too old to listen to his father."

I think about Osamu for a while. About Osamu who climbs mountains on his own, lights a campfire and prepares his meals alone, and, surrounded by clouds and light and ridgelines that I have never seen, works alone.

"I'd like to see his photos."

"Really? That will make him happy. I'll get him to call you right away."

I can tell, even from behind him, that Mr. Nishioka is smiling. I sit back in my seat. A single white contrail from a jet plane extends endlessly across the clear blue sky. Maybe I'll take a little trip with my mother when I get home, I think. Then I'll find a good hospital and start working again. Better days will surely come. After all, I am still alive.

What with not having slept the night before and the comfortable rocking of the bus, I begin to nod off as I think these things. Suddenly I hear a voice in my ear: "But before that, sweep the fallen leaves, would you? Left like that, it's not considerate of the neighbors."

I startle awake to see that the contrail has not yet vanished. In the seat beside me an old woman with her hair dyed purple is snoring. The sound of the bus engine continues smooth and uninterrupted.

I'll sweep up the leaves, light a bonfire, and roast sweet potatoes, wrapping them in damp newspaper and tinfoil. No complaints, right, Mrs. Yanagi?

"We're almost there." Mr. Nishioka lightly toots the horn. The contrail finally disappears as though melting away, yet I continue to stare up into the vault of the sky.

GAYLORD RG